ALL THAT IS UNSEEN

Sahil Bhambri

Invincible Publishers

First published in India in 2017 by Invincible Publishers

ISBN: 978-93-87328-31-0

Invincible Publishers

G-120, Sushant Lok III, Sector 57, Gurgaon-122002

Opposite Kasturba Ashram, Radaur Distt. Yamuna Nagar
Haryana - 135133

Digitally Printed at Replika Press Pvt. Ltd.

Chapter One

Autumn, not leaves but splintered feathers, waiting for a fine breeze to take them away to a new place. Atmosphere filled with a beauty of the sound of humming birds resting in the shade of a big palm tree, where sun rays scuffle hard to make their presence known on the very ground through heavy clouds, orange yet black. Strays are living their liberty on the grassy ground, with a shine in their eyes and a glow in their smiles, couples spending time together, employees with a loose tie, sipping on coffee cups, with a sense of release that they are done with their heavy duty of the day, of course – it's the weather they all enjoy after their daily duties, and yet, there was something different about the environment, as it was not the same in someone's mind, someone who was observing all the happenings of the park through a gateway.

Arav had taken an off from his daily life and stayed back home, as he was not feeling up to socialising on that beautiful day. He made a cup of coffee for himself, grabbed a book and sat near the window while reading and observing others, with a strong caffeine hit. The rush within made him want to pen down the words in the ink of seeped poetry, getting inspired by the gay nature of the park, it was laying right on the study table. He stood up, the cup of coffee still in his hands, and got a pen along with the diary he wrote in. He turned back and some of his own words caught his sight, that were pasted on the wall which had other words on them -

To die, there is always a way.

To be alive, you'll be called a survivor.

Feel it, carpe diem.

"I must've created something better," he sighed to himself.

As he made himself comfortable to write and to drink while looking though the window, he started with a line: 'Vow to me, no promises', when a loud thunder shook him. He looked out, there was no one there anymore, things he had observed before, started to disappear while he was looking at them. Rubbing his eyes, he spilled the cup of coffee over himself. 'What? Wh...what just happened in a moment, a minute before the park was crowded enough, h..h.. how come they evanesce so fast? Where have the couples gone, children, pets and everyone?' (he was screaming, but tangled within) he stammered while questioning himself, as if he was asking the window itself. Wiping his sweat, he tried hard to understand what really had happened, he got scared when he started hearing voices that were surrounding him. They seemed far at first, but then they drew closer and closer around him – "You better know that this is all your fault" – whispers in his head got louder and louder and he found himself totally out of breath, sweating, all drenched, as if he was standing in the rain. He tried hard to shout but no voice came out, he felt as if he was trying to come out from the underground, that is beneath, after a very bright flash, falling into it, falling free down from the sky. Then all of a sudden he opened his eyes to his alarm, suffocating, wet, touching himself to feel, looked out the window and then at the white ceiling, and then took a deep breath as he realised that it was just another one of his nightmares.

Shutting his alarm off, he said to himself, "Aghh, I should change my alarm tone to a holy song, maybe," and got off the bed, rubbing his eyes, partly open to see the time, it was about to be 11:40 in the morning. He woke himself up, stretching his arms wide and went to the toilet to freshen up. Staring in the mirror at himself, looking into his eyes, red, 'that was horrible', as if the life in the mirror was real – he sighed.

After being revivified, he went to the kitchen to make himself a good cup of coffee, but unfortunately, coffee capsules were finished, seemed like another nightmare, but this time it was real, "Don't kid me, I bought it just four days back, damn," but there was some powdered one on the upper shelf that he didn't like much, or it could be said that it was a reserve for a wan time like that. Bleary-eyed, he made himself a cup using the powder and after pouring it in, inclined next to the window. He glanced at the same view that he had dreamt of some minutes ago, not exactly the same, but relatable. With every sip of his coffee, he thought about the dream that he had had, questioning, lost a bit, scared.

He was deep in thought, when he received a message from Anvisha, that she would be visiting him that evening with a pastry that she made by herself, to treat him. That brought a sweet smile on his face, yes it must be, as it was his favourite, "red velvet," he said to himself while building a smile of happiness, subtly. It was 12:30 now, and having done with his cup, and his thoughts, he headed to the kitchen to make himself breakfast.

"Greek salad or sprouts...sprouts sound good." Opening the fridge door, he grabbed a packet of sprouts, it was not enough to satiate his hunger but he managed to make one adding cheese and broccoli to it. Played songs while eating his breakfast, just as every day and took an off from daily work, having done with his meal, he went to take a shower and shaved his face, yes, it had been days since he last did it, he had to go out to shop for groceries and to breathe in open air after the morning mare.

In his black denims, full sleeved white tee, a black muffler and white sneakers, he looked rustic but still capable of catching all eyes on the street. He picked up his wallet, locked the door and was all set to go.

In the cold winter gust, clouded weather, it was so serene to walk around, it felt more comfortable than being positioned at one place all day, thinking about everything that should be existing or not. Suddenly, the sounds of his surroundings started amusing him, the laughter on the street, traffic noises, the stroking break rubber with the metal of a cycle tyre, the road clock hour music. He reached one of the market stores, not the one which was close to his home, but the one a bit far away for a good walk too.

Arav first picked up the things he needed the most, coffee capsules, two boxes of capsules and some fresh mangos, berries, then vegetables, he sort of filled the cart with his needs of the kitchen, then headed to the billing counter, adding some chocolates too, well, though not some. He liked the sound that the scanner created, tiii...tiii, and placed his stuff on the counter:

"The total amount of your bag is E47.3, would you like to pay the amount by cash or card, sir?" asked the cashier.

"By card", with a polite smile, he placed a card in the machine, paid the amount, collected the receipt and left the store while humming calmness.

It was quite more windy now, while looking at the happiness of the trees on the street, sweet, he had an encounter with a busker, singing one of his favourite melodies, he stopped the moment it touched his ear drums, looking at him with mixed feelings of ecstasy and shock, he started singing along.

After spending a moment standing there, dropped 3 cents in the busker's guitar case, and left the place to go back and listen to some good music, along with writing some of the new ideas, to be penned down, for he was thinking to participate in some kind of an online competition to be featured in literary journals or writing magazines.

He reached his room, placed the groceries in their place, switched on the coffee machine, added the capsules in it, this time he took the stronger ones, he had set a reminder that Anvisha would be coming to visit him in the evening, half prepared some food for the evening for her, grabbed his cup and a diary to write verses freehand to open up his closed thoughts. It was quite cold, he flung aside his shoes, unzipped the denims and took on some shorts, making him feel easy, he took the blanket over to the sofa, which was more comfortable at times than bed, legs under blanket, after a sip, coffee on the side table.

Spending around one hour, writing and scratching at the same time, he went to his old work and started reading them. Unknowingly went into a deep sleep whilst reading his own old verses, time flowed by so fast that he didn't know that it had been more than two hours since he fell sleep.

Everywhere I am looking now,

I am surrounded by your embrace,

baby, I can feel your halo,

you are now my saving grace

His phone was ringing, Arav calmly woke up, thinking it

had only been a few minutes , looked at his coffee, cold now, searched for his phone in a hassle, it was under him, he had been sitting on the phone.

"Fuck, how come it's been that long, shit...I...I should not have fallen asleep again!! And wait? What's the matter with the reminder," he roughly asked to own.

"Hey, what's up with you, I'll be there in half an hour, just to remind you," – modulated voice.

"Oh, yeah great, I remember that, for once I can still forget about you but how could I miss my red velvet, right?"

"Of-course, yeah I know, but why is your voice so plain, were you sleeping or what?"

"Well, for a moment, yes I did sleep, but I am awake, you see," Arav said totally blank, feeling a little ashamed.

"Haha...okay, be ready, I don't want to see that sleepy ass face."

After hanging up the call, he first looked for the reminder he had fixed to keep him nudged about her arrival, he did set the reminder but unluckily, he had queued it for the hours later. "Why am I such a fool?"

The evening was so perfect in itself, there was something so romantic about that evening, he could feel it in him, as if the wind wanted to kiss him, as if the sound of the breeze was there to talk him down, he got an intuition that it was going to be so fine. Washing his face, changing clothes, not into formals, but a jeans and a black shirt, folded sleeves, all casual, he waited. Put the phone on the charge. "Knock, knock" the door sounded, just after he placed his phone on the side table of the bed, heading for the door, knowing that it must be she, he unlocked the doors' hasp, and there she was.

In her yellow tee, written 'Gentle' in the middle of a white strap, along with washed fit ripped denims, with her bracelet on her hand, sweet, white palm, black sneakers, wearing kohl in her eyes, those pretty dark black eyes, untied curly hair, great length falling down her back, and carrying her tasselled, a flower print on white with dull green straps tote bag, with a huge smile, "Hiiii," excitedly she walked in and gave him a tight hug, seemed as if it had been long.

"How do you manage to look so beautiful even in the street attire?" Arav asked while giving her a warm welcome hug.

"Ah, thank you, I know the compliment was for the thing I brought for you," she said giving a big smile and crackling laughter.

"No... no, that was for real, okay...if...you don't want to accept it," teasingly, said Arav.

She walked in, looking at the room, the surroundings, unaware of what it must be like (his place, it had been long), still having a smile, placing her bag on the bean bag, that was next to the kitchen, unzipped her bag, took out a box of pastry she had made for NAME.

"Why is the stuff dirty, your table and the sofa, don't you clean up your room?" she said to him surprised, while putting the pastry on the kitchen marble. "Why are there crushed papers, pieces of it everywhere? You used to keep your surrounding clean."

"Yeah, I know, it's a bit messy, I had a bad dream this morning, so it is all ruffled and the writing stuff, you know," he explained to her, while looking at her in a manner as if he was seeing her for the first time, he was happy.

"Oh...what dream was it? Umm, I can understand your writing stuff, how's it going?" It was clear they were meeting after a long time, knew about each other, but unaware about each other's life in the recent past.

"It is not that worthy to tell, it was just, might be some image left in my brain from the day earlier, before sleeping, of the park down there, it was about it, it was so soothing, but a minute later, suddenly everything started disappearing right in front of my eyes, and I woke up to my alarm that gave me the real shivers, that's it. Yeah, it's going pretty good, just entering in some sort of a poetry competition, that is online, it just need one piece, simple," he described to her the day and the competition bit, yes; an essence said that he was as excited as Anvisha.

"Got it, it must be horrible. And yes, give me a read of your work, I would like to." She understood him good.

Looking at the pastry, he couldn't control himself to take it out of the box and serve it, he took it from her hand and served both on a plate, their eyes spoke a lot, they wanted to share a lot, their thoughts, life, everything, yet, they were just good friend, or best.

"Damn Anvisha, it is so tasty, how do you manage to make it so perfect, thank you, I was in need of it, dire one," he said as he got the first bite in his mouth, looking into her eyes, she was still smiling, pleased to meet him, and he liked it.

"Aye, pleasure is all mine dear, glad you liked it," said she, if he told her about something new, yes, there was a lot to talk though, a lot to share.

There was something going on between them, happiness? Yes, it was happiness for being re-united after a bit long, as it seemed. So pure they were, looking and smiling at each other while eating pastry on the sofa, laughing for no reason, a typical best friend thing we can call it. A lot to share yet, they chose to share silence for a moment, after being done with their pastry. They both knew exactly where the silence was leading to while letting loose in each other's eyes, they let their eyes talk, a drop of smile on their faces, rest questions, questions they were wanting and waiting to ask to each other about each other. Yes, yes they were not more than good friends, not in a typical relationship, but in love with being together.

As a smile in coordination with the eyes started talking, sparkles in their eyes, both were listening to the muse in silence, calm and tranquil it was. After a moment of stillness and shush, they moved forward to lean, yet with a lot of questions to ask, or to share, or to let out after a sweet, lovable act, an act of love, yet as being friends, but how? They didn't know why they were doing it but it seemed like they need it, there was a craving, desiring it.

They came closer and closer till the time their eyes started to shut harmoniously and their souls met. Undergoing the taste of other lips, she bit his upper one, where he savoured the lower lip, getting frisky, no control, more assiduously pulled themselves to their bodies, she prised him to feel his body against hers by grabbing him by the back of his neck, fingers extended, wringing and clasping his hair. She made him come upon her body, desiring him, more and more and more with the act, and he seized her back, bit roughly but passionately. Unknowing of the fact that he was hurting her back, scratching marks over her love handles, but she was asking for it. It got wild when she bit his neck, with her soft pink lips, inclining his head to get to his ears, impelled to kiss over his neck.

"Don't let me dream of the fall, don't let me attend the call, the call of sin, to commit it again," she whispered to him, with unbalanced breath, as if she was asking to tighter the grip, just for the time being in that intimate act, maybe. Arav now held her face, stopped for a while, he was glancing at her with undisguised lechery, gave her a peck, and let go the hold, and delinks conspire, the interplay they had been in. Sitting at the edge of the bed, contrite gesture, clenching fist, gazed at Anvisha, as if he was about to ask now, the thing he had been waiting so long to ask, from the very moment she walked in that day. Same as him, it seemed like she too was about to start with a trail of questions, she had kept in her, to ask now.

"Have you," both arrived at the same remark, second alike.

Guffawed together, "You go first," retorted Arav.

"Haha...thank you, I was wondering if you are still with your," she was drawling, about to say further but abruptly, the phone rang all of a sudden. It was his reminder, the one he had bonded about the evening, (lost the mind again to delete it), he was living it now, he shut it off, "Sorry, my bad, what were you saying?" he asked, he wanted to know, though he knew it somehow, the question she was about to ask.

"It's okay, yeah...I was asking if you are still with your old friend, your old imaginary friend, or have you just encountered with reality?" she asked, nervous of what he would reply.

"Anvisha," he looked at her, pitiful, stopped for a second, "I never had one, are you alright, dear? Did you take a trip down your memory lane? I mean, don't you remember it was all in your head?", soothed with his voice, stammering and a bit shocked about her condition in the recent past, emphasizing on 'you', he asked, hoping she was doing good.

"Ahh, yes, I was just asking, tha...that's it, and I am totally fine now, thanks," the moment she heard that, dismayed, asked herself, 'how could I be so foolish to ask this?' or perhaps she asked because somewhere she wanted to clarify this to her own thoughts, that no, it was all in her head, that he was right, just delusions. Glanced at him, buoyantly, that he might be thinking of her as still suffering, "I am good, seriously, I just wanted to ask, to clear up my thoughts, you know, the fear," she said further, gesturing with her hands.

"Yeah, I got you, I know you, I was just concerned about your being, and how you are, dear. Are you still seeking a psychiatry treatment?" he asserted, hoping he hadn't asked something inapt.

There was a silence between them for a moment, as they wondered what to say now. A fear of something that might lead both of them to travel into the past, which might be gentle or menacing. All that happened so sudden, words and silence, both worked together as a medium of communication, sometimes the opposite, but that oppositeness of theirs' was enough to talk.

"Well, not really, it's been quite long though. My doctor said that I am out of it now...all I have to do is centralize my mind at one point, and that is through writing."

"I am glad to hear that, and would like to have a look at your writing, as we used to before."

"Oh... sure dear, I remember the time when we use to recite each other's work."

That was a conversation of fear, a fear they shared with

the other, it might have triggered the foregone pain, but they manage to face it, they were together again, knowing one won't let the other fall. It was private what they shared between them, not just the outer sight, after they were done with their questions to feel light headed, he saw the time, it was about to be nine.

"I have prepared dinner, just need to cook it, do you want me to make it now...cause I am feeling a bit hungry," said Arav.

"Oh, I know you are always a hungry ass, have you really prepared the meal, I am so pleased...thanks," she claimed. "Should we go outside for dinner? I mean yes, if you want to make it at home... I am fine with that too; you have concocted a dinner, no...we should stay at home." Clearly she was so confused, but she respected him, so she decided to stay there, despite her wanting to go out.

He knew that she wanted to go out for dinner. "Did you seriously think that on such a beautiful day we were going to stay in here? I think you are right, we should go out, and don't worry about the food, I'll make it for myself for breakfast...I am clever you see," he knew exactly what she wanted, and he too wanted some fresh air to breathe, he always did, as he was always confined within himself. Knowing that he wanted to write, and he could only write the times he got some fresh environment.

Anvisha filled with excitement, she was always excited, asked him if he wanted sushi, their favourite, they couldn't really remember when was the last time they had it together, of course a long time ago. Getting ready to leave for the beautiful diner, he was all set to go, she was already prepared. Locked the door after picking up the essentials, walked down using staircase, as the lift was at the 8th floor, and was taking a bit too long to come down, walked the street with a perfect breeze, moonlight bouncing back, soothing the surroundings, calm. yet thunderous.

Heading towards the convent garden by using the tube, the feeling was so perfect, it was in the air, the minty green stars. Talking about the things they wanted to talk about, the condition of Anvisha, her personal life for a bit, and the same with her, as she was concerned about him, about his life, about him, if he was out of the chains or still confined.

They reached the convent garden, sharing their positive vibes and words, what ere awaited for a long time, walks in the sushi restaurant, always clashing onto the same ones, their preferences were so similar, but they couldn't order the same again and again. California rolls, along with salmon, the sweet one and the tuna with prawns, they ordered. Spending some quality time together, they couldn't stop talking, still a lot to share, to talk what was really left, left somewhere in the bright breeze, or the darkness of the truth they didn't want to come up with, at that moment, maybe the next time they would meet, as now she was back staying in London.

Their sushi arrived after a bit of wait, the place was crowded. Having finished with their dinner, and the time they were spending together, Anvisha was about to leave for her place.

"It was a perfect evening after that long, really, but I think it is quite late now, I should leave, and I am sure we are meeting in some days, again."

"Yes, it was. I don't remember the last time I had this much fun with someone. Thanks for your visit, and yeah we are meeting for sure, how are you going to get back, by bus?"

"Ah, yeah, by bus, it would be great by bus, it will hardly take twenty to thirty minutes from here, thank you, we'll plan the meet in this week again, yeah."

"Sure, take care, give me a ping once you reach," he said, giving her a warm hug, he didn't want to leave her, but he had to. He spentall his time alone and when he met someone, it was so precious for him, and so hard to depart with them till the next time.

"Haha, Arav, I am not a kid, thank you, bye, take care, dear," she held onto him the same way, she was meeting him after long, maybe a year, and it was the same with her, as her condition was pretty serious, which had improved a lot, but still, for a person like her, it was always hard, again when she'd get back to her home, she'd be alone again, till the next morning when she would meet her other friends, no one like him though.

After she took the bus, for he had stayed with her till the time she got the bus, he headed toward his home, smiling to himself, remembering the day's talks they had had, and how perfect it was, how he really liked it after a time. Took out his phone, he did not have his diary or stuff, opened the notes and added:

"Lived in the dark,

for the solitude phrase: i meet,

knowing the desire of hurt,

hoping the pain would greet.

and again, let me fly,

don't leave: for another goodbye,

in the land like never,

let me say my unseen why's."

He wandered through the cold street, (not going straight away to his home), to clear his mind of all the ongoings surrounding him, he did not know what it must feel like when someone looks for a reason directly, instead of a solution. "Don't run, don't run dear," he overheard, walking down the street, turned to his left, there was a guy whom a girl was trying hard to control, seemed like he was overly drunk. 'But it's not even the weekend today,' he said to himself and started walking towards them to help.

"Is everything alright?" he looked into the lady's eyes and asked.

"Oh yeah, it's just everyday's story, thanks for your concern and stopping by," she replied with a smile full of sorrow, as if it was her daily struggle to deal with. Saying "Take care," he left.

Arav headed on his way back, the moment he reached, standing on the street of his house, suddenly everything started to amaze him, from the street lights to the crowd of the Saturday night clubs. He was so tangled to be entangled in himself that he couldn't understand what and why he was thinking about, did he really exist?

Questioning himself about everything, whether it belonged to him or not, it started bothering him, the amazement of his own existentialism, or maybe he was over-thinking and joining up all the terms that he had read. The night was finally about to fall, to sleep.

Nihilist in his room, after being on the street the previous night, his reminder for the morning popped up, of seeing his landlord to pay the rent.

Chapter Two

Woke up to a beautiful morning of another day, with the birds chirping around his window, there was no sun that day, he was getting disturbed by the reminder which was popping up again and again. Frustrated, he looked at his phone, and realized that he was screwed yet again the other way. He always tried to rest, or to find for himself what had gotten lost somewhere, something came by his way to take his state; still he painted a smile on his face every day, no matter if it was a storm or another mare, or the fragrance of a rose with its darkest side.

He didn't want to see his landlord that morning, for he would make him stay for some talk and coffee, "I'll meet them in a day or two, not now", he makes an online transaction for his rent into the landlord's bank account and makes a call to them.

"Hey Uncle James, sorry, I can't meet you today. I've made an online transaction of the rent, just check for a message from the bank, and I will surely try visiting you this week," he said, guessing that they might have felt bad, for they lived with sheer joy whenever he visited, but he had to do other work that day.

"Hi Arav, Mrs. Walsh this side, I'll let him know about it, but why are you not coming? I wanted to meet you, it's okay if you have some work in your hand, but meet me soon, okay?"

"Oh, hi aunt, yes sure, I will meet you soon, I've just got some work, take care, bye," feeling a bit light headed, with a sense of guilt, as they had been expecting him. He had great landlords, they were so simple and pure, an old couple, who loved each other so much and were always eager to hear stories from his life.

He got off from the bed, into the morning light, after having had a long night that he struggled to sleep through, turned on the machine, put the capsule in, poured the coffee into his whitish blue cup, and added some water into the machine's water depot for next time, looked at the time, it was 11:40 A.M., thought about the competition he was writing for, he had to send in his entry for poetry. Arav so wanted to join this competition, in order to reach out to a wider readership and to see if he was even capable of winning the competition by any chance, except for the fact that he wrote good but never liked his own work. After his coffee, he went to shower to start afresh, and send his entry for the poetry competition.

He stepped out of the shower refreshed, humming to himself, wearing only his briefs even though it was cold, but he didn't feel cold unless the temperature was below 4*C, threw away the meal that he had prepared the night before, wasted, made himself pancakes with chocolate and some berries for breakfast, sat on the bed, not the sofa today, it was so untidy, covered under a lot of stuff, though he loved to keep his surroundings clean, sometimes he felt too lazy to even move his leg. Turned on the laptop, opened the mail to write them, the submission. He had already written a piece of poetry on his phone the night before when he was struggling hard to sleep, night was the best time for him to rant his scream into words, or to write the feelings, he had done the same, he did the same every night. Arav saw the deadline he had received through mail which was for the next day and the result were to be out within a week, and the winning writer's Arav was to be announced on the site as well as personally through call, and it would be published in their journals, yes, it was quite a famous journal he has put himself in the competition for.

Picked up his phone from the side table of the bed, opened the notes where he had written a piece the last night, and in the mail box, he started,

OXYMORON:

Incarceration needs an obscure voice,
Agony smiled to ambivalent cries.
Dreaded life to commit sin,
If an esoteric truth lives within.

Touch: let me live death,
Please hear me, the voided breath.
Realness rued over chicanery,
Hope clasped upon the dead fairy.

Slithered, the time I need love,
Shadows trusted an evil dove,
Love confides lies in the dark,
Belief hung fire to embark.

Feel: let me cry a smile,
Tears lived in exile.

Substance of ruthlessness made a dune,

Wolf howls again to the moon.

With mixed feelings he had written this poetry the previous night, with a lot of feelings and thoughts of solitude and existentialism, even he didn't know why he had written it, all that he knew was the title, the term - Oxymoron, one of his favourite terms, which amazed him all the time. He sent the mail, hoping they would like it, but whatever, he had ranted his words.

A believer of truth too, sometimes speaks the most lies, this way or the other. Beneath, all of us know the truth. Truth, truth, truth –say it as many times as you want, after all it will remain just a term at the end of the day.

"Frozen breath, cold death, grey pain, no merriment, who to trust?" while putting his laptop back on the table, he laid his sight over his writing on the wall, to the right of the window, opposite the sofa. A room full of his own philosophies, and the other writers' quotes. He recited the line again and it gave him real chills.

" brave, I am,

for the days of paleness,

dreaming all the might,

touching my inner mess."

He added further, the lines he had just recited, as if it was meant to be complete only after these lines. Arav said it out loud, the words, slowly, by feeling each alphabet over his tongue, he wasn't yet done with the morning's caffeine consumption and made himself another cup of coffee, briskly this time, as if he needed it, the real need for anther caffeine hit, but why? Was he trying to run away from the fact that he has trapped in the dark side of reality? Or maybe he didn't want to accept the fact that yes, he couldn't get over his own thoughts, syllogism, he was trying to come out of his own concept of it -

"Alive goes to dead; dead live in graves and being alive therefore, everyone's dead."

He didn't know what was right anymore, he was so done with the realness of the dark light of the day, being so helpless, he wanted to scream at his confusion or at his inner thoughts, in order to let go of the very harsh reality he was living, he took a novel from the shelve and started reading it to forget about it, or to widen his thoughts, questions. The book was by Albert Camus, whom he admired – The Stranger.

After reading through some pages, when he felt relieved, he put the book back on the shelf, while placing it back, he saw something he had been running away from, maybe.

Being confined in his own league, there was something he feared the most, what was it? Why was he always out of breath? What was it on that shelf that he was so scared of, that seemed to have remained unopened for months? His breath got heavier as he laid his sight over the old diary that was now placed at the very top of the shelf, he reached up with his body to grab it, the heavy old brown diary with a finger print engraved onto the very middle of the front face, and with a quote on the back cover which read, "Unchain the fly, to unbound the cries."

Holding the old diary in his hands, he looked at it for long, still. He travelled back into his memory, seeing dark everywhere, but with a dot of light, an illusion, like water in a desert.

Sweating, he didn't know what he was thinking about, he was blank, certainly empty inside, his sweat dropped onto the diary, a blob in the middle, repelling the dirt that had collected over it, it made him delink from the isolation that he had created around himself while being lost upon seeing that diary, he didn't even try to open it, shivering a bit, thinking whether to even open it or not, but ended up placing it back. "Not now please, don't make me lost it, I'll surely open you in sometime, it's just not the time now for you to fuck my life again, the secrets you carry in you are hell for me sometimes, don't make me remember the worst, the past form what I have stepped forward," Arav guffawed to himself, looked at the mirror next to the bed, stared at himself, and said, "You, yes you are illusionary, you are a reflection, that's it, don't try to confront with reality, look inside, that's the real you." After saying this, he sat on the edge of the bed and thought what that was? Why did he say those words to himself? Was it coming again, for he felt the anger in the whispery low note of his voice? Turned to the window, looked at the park, as if he was searching for someone there, moving his eyes, wider, he was looking for someone, but whom?

It was quite windy outside, he went closer to the environment while staying where he had been earlier, listening closely to the rustling of the surrounding, the trees, the birds, everything but still, he was precariously looking for something, someone out there. And there he spotted the one, an old hand in its great disguise again. Wearing a round hat on his head, a dull black jacket over a white polo tee, a blackish grey jeans with the same old boots, an overall rugged appearance. He might look poor at times, but he was a magpie who had seen the harsh time. On finding him, he felt a relief in his chest, released from his dark thoughts, he muffled to himself-

"Here he stands again, sauntering around in search of another me, he must have guided a lot of people after me, still the thirst in his eyes to take someone outside from their problems can clearly be seen from that far. I should go to him now; it is the time again, maybe."

Wearing his clothes a bit hurriedly, he left his house for the park to meet the old person walking in disguise. Arav reached the park, searched for him, "Where has he gone, he was right there, under the tree," looked around, unstable, uneven heart rate, starting to get a bit pale. Suddenly he heard a humming sound, trying to recognise that tone, he looked to his right; there he was on a bench, humming an unknown melody, with a feather in his hand, white, he was staring at it, smilingly, as if he was talking to it. Taking big steps, Arav walked swiftly towards him.

"Hey sir, do...do you remember me?" he asked with a smile, a bit scared whether he remembered him or not, his breath grew rough.

"Hey there, son, ahh," he paused for a while as if trying to recognise him, "Oh yes, of course I remember you, you haven't changed a bit, how are you son?" he said, still sitting on the bench with that feather in his hand, that same old manly voice, strong and silvery, yet smoky.

"Oh, how glad I am, you do." With an ease, he looked up at the sky and breathed, "I...I...I am fine ,sir." He couldn't say anything else, his voice was strangled.

"Oh child, I wish you were," he said wiggling his head, with a mysterious smile, gesturing through his eyes, "Come and sit with me, and share all your vague thoughts," and patted on the bench next to himself.

He, Arav, knew from that very moment that he, the old man in disguise, was going to take him out again, like he did some time ago, last year, maybe. But why did he call him old man in disguise? Was he really in disguise of someone else? He sat with him, looking at the ground, with a fallen head, tired of running from him, looked at the old man and said, "How do you know about it? Like you did earlier too?" he asked the old man bewildered, he seemed to know everything about him, even before listening to him.

"Haha," he tittered and glanced at him, saying, "I don't know anything, it's you who does," leaving Arav even more confused, he started looking at the feather.

"But…but, sir. Ahh, I don't know, why you holding and staring at the feather, what is it, you seem to know everything, but you are again making me more confused about myself," his tone became more irritating, as he didn't seem to understand anything.

The old man looked at him, smiled, and taking that feather up to the level to his eyes, holding it so carefully, he said, "You see this feather, it is probably the lightest thing you'll ever see, and the weakest by its appearance, but still my son, when it falls, it make its way to the ground by not getting hurt. The winds might blow all of a sudden and change its way to the ground, and sometimes it might not even fall but get stuck somewhere, but it still manages to come to rest, floating in its own muse, braving all the dares. The owner of the feather may have lost it or abandoned it, but once it's gone, the bird can't ever fix it, and the feather still lives. It is the same with our lives; it is as weak as a quill and as strong as its will. Like a feather, our lives too are so delicate, precious, beautiful; let it all happen, let everything comes your way; you have to make it through, like it did. The bird and this quill are more resilient than we think they are," the old man said while staring at the feather and glancing at Arav. Smiling that tasted storm, he added, "You are brave, I don't know what your are undergoing, but I know my son, you are brave."

He was lost somewhere in his words, the lesson he had just taught him without even knowing his condition, what he was feeling inside, nothing, comforting him with his words, as if he belonged to him only. Maybe, that was the reason that Arav called him 'an old man in disguise', disguise of an angel, and disguise of someone who belonged to him alone, who came by when he needed him the most.

The very first time when he had met the old man at Hide Park, when he had been living a song of melancholy and experiencing despair, he was standing still and looking at the park's fountain for two hours without moving, he was so lost, not knowing that it had been for hours that he was still and lost in the muse of it, empty, blank. This old man had been discerning him for long, as the old man was there with his dog, playing and resting. He walked up to him and distracted him from the link that he had made with isolation, while being in reality. He had asked him if he wanted something, Arav had looked at him, the old man seemed poor, but he was not for he had taken him to a coffee shop nearby and brought a cup each for himself and for Arav. He was an actual gentleman who didn't like to attract attention, but only to help, like he did. He had indulged with Arav in a conversation and Arav had told him about his life, he then had given him a lesson saying, "Don't get stuck in your problems, they are temporary, if you want to be, then tie yourself with the dare to touch the ascent."

They had spent some time together, and he thanked him for the help, he didn't realise then, that he had done him a great help by listening him out.

Then after some time, he met the same old man in the park again where they were now, he seemed happy with his dog, playing with others too, laughing with joy, with an old smile of experience. There he came to know that he came there every 3 days, to feed the other dogs and to help someone like him. Arav remembered all this, but not the time and not his words, that had helped him with his despair.

Coming back to reality from his memory lane, he looked at him; the old man was staring at him mysteriously, and giggled a bit as he said, "Where have you been? I am still here, you are not alone, when you feel that you are, just look at the sky and get lost in the depth of it, like a rollercoaster ride in some amusement park, but my boy, this ride is going to be the real ride, not the ride you know, but you feel it, feel it inside you. I think you should see it by yourself, if you can't find the way, I will be here to hold your hand and unchain you to pull you up to the bright world.

Apparently, he knew it himself that he was the only one who could help. The oscillation of his own thoughts and the ride back into the past while living in the present was killing all of what may be his future to survive. The old man and Arav completed sharing their link and the old man got up, giving his feather to Arav and said, "It's time for me to leave I guess, to leave you strangled in yourself, so that you foster a wall that no one can climb but you." He, Arav, thanked him and looked at the feather that he had lent to him, and thinking about the delicateness of it, he left the park to go back to his room.

There used to be a difference between LIFE and FICTION, which had vanished from his life when he turned his back to the present, in favour of the past, just to have some good days for the first time, maybe.

Always wondering what life is, living in a dreamland most of the time, he had always asked himself why he lived in an illusion which he hated himself it. His answer to it was that sometimes all we need is a hope, all the rejoinder lays beneath, but hope at times is the best thing to save oneself. Both work parallelly, reality and imagination, that is – life and fiction. When reality hurts us, we turn our backs on it, and live in imagination, when imagination becomes too illusionary, we go back to reality. None of us is still, stable in one's own league, instead of finding out the root of our problems, we run after the solution itself, so how could one stay stable? Human race is corrupted.

He head towards a nearby book store instead of his room, to buy a thriller book, that had come to his mind all of the sudden, to divert his mind and to drift to somewhere else. He visited the nearby book store, soothing atmosphere, the ambience, green, blue, and white in colour, the walls, withsome faces on it, at the fiction section there was two faces imprinted on the wall, one was laughing and the other concealing cries, one over the other, and the mystery section had a face on which the mouth was upwards and the eyes downwards, he entered the store, not many people were around the corner, stepped towards the thriller section in search of the book he wanted to read – 'Before I Go to Sleep' by S.J. Watson, not being able to find the book in any of the shelves at the section, he hoped for it to be there at the very bottom shelve, on his knees, he sat on the floor, searching but couldn't find, just as he got up disappointed, he caught a sight of the book, held by someone else.

White sneakers, torn shorts, toned thighs, basic denim tee with 'Day dreams, but the night shows' written on the front, long curly brunette hair, white hands holding that book, specs hiding her bluish eyes, a smile with which she read the cover. He was approximately two feet from her, looking at the book and the girl. Caught, she exuberantly turned the book and got to see a shadow near her, still, a face it was, she turned to her left whilst flicking her hair back, setting her spectacles, as they was about to fall, looked at him a bit bewildered and giggled, that was the time when he first noticed her pinprick beauty mark.

"Hey," she said with a smile, "Are you looking for this book?"

"Ah," he knew he would stammer nervously, "Well yes, I...I was looking for just this one and I don...don't think there are any more copies left," he finally said while looking at and getting lost in her beauty, her voice, polite as a humming bird's, was amusing.

"Ohh...oh...I got it," the confident she wore was sensational, "Do...do you want this one, cause I was ju...just reading it," she said, offering him the book with her right hand. She is something joyous, a beauty with a pure heart, Arav felt.

"If you don't mind, because I was particularly looking for this book and sorry for staring like that, no offense," said Arav, unruffled this time.

"Here you go, happy reading," giddily she replied, while proffering the book to him. "I am a reader too and I know what you must have felt a minute ago by seeing it in my hand." Giving him the book, she bided a hand shake that very moment.

"Oh...thanks a lot for this," he said happily.

"Nasia, it was pleasure to meet you," he noticed a bit of excitement in her.

"Arav, same here," he said shaking her hand, sharing a smile, after which, she left. While walking away, she turned back and said, "Take care." He said the same.

In that moment of encounter, he felt something mighty inside him, that mightiness was a relief after meeting her, Nasia. She was so pure inside out, he still stood there where she had left him, watched her leaving and after a moment, went to the counter to make the purchase.

Leaving the store, humming, he felt a shivering excitement inside. Walking back to his room, a sweet outburst of wind gently touched his face as if it wanted to talk a saga. There was an an eye-catching advertisement board on the street which caught his sight as it was so bright. "The Art Fair," he read. "Tomorrow at Southwark row, Blaze of Art." It was quite far from his place but he had to go there, for the place, art fairs were always good and that's what he liked them the most, or maybe, they were one of his favourite. "I must go," he mumbled.

After twenty minutes of walk, he reached home, in that twenty-minutes he had been to many places while staying at one, a lot of thoughts he had travelled through, the very thought of the result of the competition started to amaze him, and the next day's art fair too, for him it would be fun.

He had spent around three hours outside, first he had met the old man, then the book store and then the walk down home. While thinking about the next day's fair, he felt like meeting his landlords, for they had been waiting for him.

He decided to meet them before going to the fair, he made a call to them to tell them he would visit them in the morning the next day.

"Hii.." he paused to hear from them first, "Uncle James, I'll be coming to meet you tomorrow morning, is that okay?"

"Arav...how are you my son, I got your message, it's okay dear," he took a second break before proceeding further and said, "It would be better if you come the day after tomorrow because your aunt and I are going to visit our grandson tomorrow, but that doesn't mean that your coffee is not pending, meet us soon.".

"Oh...okay sir, yes sure, I'll try to visit you then, take care." He was too desirous of meeting them soon to hear the uncle's new story.

Before making himself slouch on the bed, he had to make himself a cheese sandwich with brown bread, and he had all the ingredients in stock to make it now. After making one, he went to bed, placed the plate on the pillow and awakened his phone to check his mail. He ate the sandwich, resting and thinking whether to read that book by Albert Camus any further, the one he had been reading earlier that morning. He spent the rest of his day in bed, relaxing and listening to music online, browsing randomly and searching for new tunes to make a new playlist.

Right before going off to sleep, his thoughts started haunting him about the night to come, how would he survive the night again? Every flashback from the day started appearing right in front of his eyes. From the diary he saw in the morning, where the day had started, the diary that had stroked him up, then suddenly the image shifted to the book store and the quote he had read on the girl's tee – "Day dreams, but the night shows".

What does the night show? Why does the day dream, the show of the dream embarked in his mind, he forgot about the girl he had met, but not the quote, was he even aware of the day that he lived today? What was there in the night, why did he fear the dark and still loved the concept of dark, and not light, or colours. Why did he not like the taste of colours and yet, love Art. Arav was a person of mystery living inside, unbounded by the reality of outside.

" Whenever the night arrives,
birth takes disguise,
in the dark; unfelt corner,
tries to create; light of no rise,
for to live again, minty pain,
and to survive; words of own."

Arav's fear of the night, the bright nightmare of Anvisha, when she found some of his imagination in the light, while living in concealed black thoughts herself, amazed every wordy world. Before going off to sleep, all the memories of Anvisha came to him again out of nowhere, for he was concerned about her for no reason, all this was striking while he fought against his sleep and the night.

Chapter Three

On the muse of birds wimbling around, and the morning light making shadows evanesce, he woke up to another beautiful day, but what had happened the previous night was a bit terrible. 'He sleeps, but he never rests', the story of every night took with it to haunt him with new daunt.

He woke up before the alarm, despite having stayed up late the previous night night, craving art; he would wake a million stars to his untold lullaby. Art for him was something mighty in its own, it talked in several ways, showed the reality and the very inside of an artist. He couldn't draw himself but tried and ended up creating a mess that was understandable only to him. Excited, a new spark of happiness to see the fair with talented beings around him, he'd get a lot to write, he said to himself.

Enlivened enough, Arav got off for a shower, in a jiffy got ready, he didn't even make himself breakfast, for he would have it on his way to the Southwark, with no interval he put his clothes on, the ones he had chosen the previous night for today. A baby pink shirt tucked in black jeans, white sneakers, tuned hair, he was onto something formally casual. Wallet, the phone, and a pen in royal blue colour, his favourite. Left home at 11:30 in the morning and took a bus to the tube station.

When he got off the bus for the tube, he noticed a bakery, and went in to have something to eat before reaching there, ordered an avocado salad with extra olives and a double espresso for the day's charge. He sat there for around twenty minutes and in that time, went through the details of the fair, it was to start at 2. A bit chilled out about getting there on time, as there would not have been much crowd in the very beginning, it was a Sunday too, so people would have liked to arrive late, but not like him, an art enthusiast. After spending some time on social media and having done his breakfast, he left the bakery for the tube and took one to Southwark. There were plenty of people in the tube who seemed to be going to the fair, just an intuition he got, or perhaps his excitement for the fair was taking over his thinking, having lost it.

"In a vivacity; deteriorated
i stand,
hollowness; wasted land.
Crumbled with the pain,
ache in the voice,
asking to die, with no choice.
O'my custodian; nature
let me love you,
before they kill me too,
let's turn blue.

Thunderous inside, with the same artistic feel about god's vivacity, nature, what has been destroying for the so called human means, he wrote with a heavy chest. It was just two stations away, asked for directions from the one sitting next to him, "After getting out, make sure the exit is to your left, head straight, and then take the first left, it would be to your right, after about six minutes of walk," the one claimed, sitting next to him, Arav was curious to know if the person was coming to the fair too, when he asked it, "oh...no, no, I have my shop here, just five minutes of walk from the art gallery, utility shop, you may get whatever you want, and in its most unique way, that's our motive."

"Oh, great, I must visit you soon then, I will try to come after the fair if I can, thanks," he remarked, a bit released now, knowing the way to the fair, and it was about to be 2:10 now. "It was nice to meet you," same here, the man claimed with a delightful smile.

Came out from the station and headed in the same direction, as told by the man in the tube. After five minutes of walk, he started seeing a crowd, elegant, artist, it said on their faces. He stoped there for a moment to observe his surroundings, "They must all be artists, and very few of them would be viewers like me," he mumbled inwardly and calmly. The pure cold breeze and a tranquil entrance into the fair got him, with the red carpet. What he saw while walking toward the entrance was two persons standing and checking paper like things in the hands of all the ones who were entering. He approached them, "Sir, your pass please?" they asked.

He didn't know what pass they were talking about, "A pass? For what? I don't have any," he felt totally muddled. A pass? What must it be for, the entry?

"Sir, for the entry, didn't you register yourself online for the fair?" a lady in black asked him, while the other gentlemen gained access.

"Register, no, I didn't, I didn't even know about this thing, I saw your poster on the street and made myself come here, that's it." He was starting to get a bit nervous, thinking whether he'd get an entry or not just because of the damned online registration.

"Oh...no problem sir, don't be worried, we've got you. In that case, I'll make you register at the counter there, it's just a formality, sorry, I can't help this," she claimed, feeling his craving for the fair perhaps, so she did not waste even a second more and took him to the counter.

Arav was looking at the entry; he observed a lot of people while ambling towards the counter, hoping it wouldn't take too much time. It was so calm, the atmosphere, he was not in yet, but the vibes were so pure, a bit suffocated crowd, still not all.

"Hey Aria, can you help him out with the registration please, he didn't know about it, and yes, quickly please," the lady asked the one sitting at the counter.

"Hi...yeah sure," she said, wearing a big beautiful smile, as she was there to help and liked her job. "Okay, you can go back to your place now, I got him," she said further. "Thanks dear," turning back to Arav, "Have a great day, Aria will help you out, it'll only take some minutes," the lady remarked. Arav thanked her and sat there, looking at Aria, she was doing something on her laptop.

Hi...sorry for the delay," she paused for a moment, "Let's get this done fast, I don't want you to be late. Can you please fill out this form for me, it will hardly take a minute or two," Aria offered him her laptop to fill a form, Arav took her laptop and started reading the details to be filled – Name, age and sex, address, contact details, reason to be at the fair and the source, it said, he filled it. The reason section got him, he was amazed to see that on the form, it had amazed him about how important it was to be filled by the visitors, the reason why they liked art, what was it. Being a writer, he respected it and wrote his reason.

After completing the form, he gave the laptop back to her. After that she made a pass for him to access the fair, and was cross checking his details, just like that. "What...that is just amazing," she said in a wavered tone, running her inner wows while looking at him.

"What...what is it?" He was confused.

"Your reason for coming to the fair is just wow, I...I mean beautiful, we always look forward to someone like you, the thirst for art, I am really impressed," Aria remarked in an amazing way.

"Oh...haha...now I know," he felt relieved and happy to know that she respected that, "It's just in me, I am here to explore and to open my lost or hidden thoughts, to write," he added further.

"Write...am I talking to a writer right now?" she said with her bug eyes, after a second, "I am really happy to meet you then, it is beautiful, isn't it? I think you must go inside now, I would like to meet you after the fair if I can, surely," she said as her phone rang, perhaps related to her work, Aria wanted to talk more, but couldn't, that was not the right time, she told Arav to go in, she wanted to know about him more, next time, maybe.

"Haha...thank you for showing this much respect, Aria, and I really like your name, it's a muse...haha," he looked into her eyes, feeling that she wanted to talk more but couldn't at thay moment, "Sure, we'll meet, thank you once again." She handed over his pass to him, he left for the entrance of fair, excited, hailing a new glow.

Strolling towards the entry again, the lady passed him a smile and led the way into the fair. The time he got in, he felt lost, as if he was trying to breathe, to fill his lungs with the smell and voice of art. Oil paintings, sketches, colours, a pottery painting, dry-points, he was surrounded by all that. He looked at each and every piece that the walls carried, showing another world to him. Calm urbane music marked a smooth undertone for the viewers. He started looking around and tried to know the meaning of the pieces he saw, from beneath, the feel to make one, he was all about the emotions of the artist while making the art he was seeing then.

'All Reticent Thoughts' was Art for him, the real meaning of it. Again the thoughts of the rubbish world started hitting him, hard this time, questioning himself about the existentialism of one's own self, while keeping in mind the famous play – Waiting for Godot, like the men in the play who were waiting for someone to meet with, not even knowing who Godot is, or anything about the person at all, but they kept on waiting to meet the one, and after all the happenings in between, the play ends without them having met with this unknown figure. But as being a play on existentialism and totally absurd, he still managed to find reason in it, as the characters intervened each other. Like the play, while looking at a painting in four colours – green, light blue, orange and yellow, making the sky by hiding the sun and the clouds. There was a tree, standing tall, but the strange colour of the tree, black, took Arav somewhere into the deepness of it, right next to the black tree, there were three persons carrying each other, and the shadow of two gripping them. It was not brush, but fingers that were used in this painting. A red flowing river just behind the tree left him in questions. From where had this red occurred, and why had the orange sky taken over the blueness, falling down onto the river.

The red eye,

orange blue,

shivering the path; dark hue,

whispering to cry,

bloodshed, bloodshed,

earlier, the murder of inner; she flew.

In the green land,

hate she drew,

love touching the pink; she grew.

Who must 'she' be? What was going on in his mind? Maybe she was the one who murdered the reality, falsity, the time she touched the bright hue, pink, by coming out from the dark side of her own, she met love, she was the artist of the painting, as he read the name and signature mentioned at the bottom of the painting. Looked around but found no one to whom the painting belonged, though it belonged to everyone if it was in the exhibition there, but the one who owned it must have been busy in taking her admirers.

Sauntering with a thirst to find something more mesmerizing, he gaped at some more pieces, some were about the racism, hard work, alienation, whereas some had sexual elements, hatred. He drank in the mist of the ambience and the gaiety of the aura, what a pleasure it was for him to be there, when he found himself standing in front of an oil painting and a sketch right next to it, a guy holding a pen in his hands and a diary on his lap, looking at birds flying, with hills behind, that were so soothing. Arav turned to his right, another wall of art, he walked towards it and stood still whilst observing something mighty, or so he felt it was.

A shouting man shedding tears of blood, and a naked lady, with a broken piece of mirror in her hand, sharp and pointed, holding the edge of it to her throat and with the other hand covering her breast, standing before him, laughing. Both were under a dark sky with some stars, and a shadow of a hand grabbed the waist of the lady. Behind the shouting man, there was a boy with his finger painted, tearing apart the head of his teddy. There was a second lady figure too, if one was to look at it closely, hidden, painted below the breast, over the belly of the first naked lady, this one was on her knees, screaming, with her hand tied.

Somehow, it left Arav in tears, he cried unknowingly while looking at the painting. He had been trying to grasp the depth of it, or perhaps he had already done that. In his mind, it was all revolving, so heavy, like a wave of the sea, coming but not returning back. He tried to reach his hand to his face, to really feel if he existed, it was all coming back to him, suddenly he started thinking if Anvisha had really visited him that evening, or if he had really met the old man. With open eyes, he underpinned a blurry delusion of the cliff, where he looked down, it was so deep, he couldn't even tell if the bottom existed or not, he didn't want to see who was standing at his back, as he could only see the shadow that got bigger and bigger with every second, finding no choice, he jumped.

When he jumped off the cliff, he felt a hellish whirlwind, he got called back to the reality just then, as if by being hit hard on a trampoline. He found tears on his face, increased heart rate, rushing inside, and again in front of that painting. He wiped his face, and tried to come back from the place he had been lost in, just a moment ago. Arav must have got a lot to write now, for sure, new concepts, theories, ideas. Inertly, there was someone who had been noticing him, maybe for some minutes, he felt the presence of someone, eyeing him down, and he came to his consciousness and looked back. A smile carrying questions looked at him, as if she was trying to reckon him. He didn't know how to react, glancing with a frown at her, feeling as if he had already met her.

"Hi…sorry, but are you alright?" she asked and paused for a moment, "Aren't you the same guy from the bookstore?"

"Hey," he said nervously, "yeah, I...I am, just went a bit too deep looking at this piece." He pointed at the painting. "Hey...yeah...I remember you, you are the one who gave me the book," confidently this time, a bit happy to see her again, "It's nice to meet you, again."

"Haha...yeah...it's nice to meet you too, and here of all places, I am glad," she asked further with interest in her eyes, "You like art?"

"Oh yes...I do, a lot actually," he gestured with excitement, "I was so lost, and this piece of art is the best I've come across in the fair till now," he looked into her eyes, "I...I was really grasping my breath, haha...what about you? You like art too? Great, look at this one," he told her.

"An unruffled storm," she read the name of the piece, "It's alluring, yet dark. The artist must have undergone something immense," squinting her eyes and tilting her head, "Don't know, it's great, but will take time for anyone to understand the piece, but I think you did it, if you noticed the lady beneath."

"Yeah, true...oh...you have seen the painting already? I wonder why there's no information about the artist, they must have forgotten to add the description maybe," he said confusedly.

"They might have forgotten to add...haha...I have already seen this one...well, it's quite strange, isn't it?" she sighed.

"What...what is it?"

"That we are meeting for the second time, and we met both times at our favourite places, right?" she said while looking around.

"That's true, I got you," he stood still. "It's a fortuity, a beautiful one," he said, calmly looking at her.

There was a silence while they shared their words, but what was it really? Why did the silence choose to occur in that perfect ambience and aura when they had meet again? Her phone rang all of sudden, distracting both of them. "I have to take this call, I'll see you in a while for sure," she said. She didn't want to turn her back to him, she wanted to say something, but the call interrupted her. What must it be?

"Oh...sure, no problem, I'll be here," he said on the phone, downheartedly.

Arav glanced at the painting one last time after Nasia left and looked for more art next to it and in the other halls, he was calm in tranquillity, and it was so perfect when he took out his phone to note down his very thoughts, the thoughts he endured from the painting he had just discerned.

"Perceive the truth,

the moon, the sun, all the lights or the dark, to learn.

In a dream we live, or a hope we create,

the unlearnt will come, and stop your way."

"Hey...how's it going?" He got interrupted by a familiar voice while he was writing. He looked up, it was Aria.

"Oh...hi...yeah...it...it's going great, I was just writing

something," he said, trying to grip onto his thoughts, so as not to let them go due to this sudden conversation, but they did.

"Ah...I see...good...I'll surely read your words once," she said with a certain curiosity in her. "I just got free from my work, another person took the counter, have you seen that art?" she asked, pointing to the right, where he had just met Nasia.

"Yeah...I just saw that, it is beautiful. That might be an inapt word to describe it...actually every piece here is."

"Ahan... great, have you seen 'An unruffled storm'?"

"To be honest, that was the best I've come across," he said, looking at her a bit demented, "but why did you specifically mention it?

"Wow," she said excitedly, "That piece of art is actually by a close friend of mine, she is amazing...have you...have you met her yet?" she asked, wearing a great smile on her face.

"Amazing," he said surprised, "No, there was no description of the artist there, I have been searching for the one too," he claimed.

"Oh haha...okay...sorry for that...she always removes her description from her pieces...to remain hidden, it's just so her...it's okay, she is there," Aria said, indicating towards the entrance. "Come with me...I will introduce you to her, writer."

"Haha, sure," he said, curious to find out who the artist was, who tried to hide herself.

While following Aria, he got lost in questions, and the thoughts that had been gripping him to write something down, got lost in the conversation. Watching other people look at paintings and sketches, he questioned himself, did he even see something, or was he even there, at the fair? Not knowing about anything, he blindly followed Aria towards the hidden artist, a strange rapture growing inside him. There and then, the concept of dark started hitting him; he could see where he was going by following her to the artist, but with an imagery of dark. "There she is...meeting her clients," Aria said, gesturing at her.

He looked at the lady, her back was towards them, he tries to recognise the way her hair flowed and her waist, he had seen her somewhere for sure, he said within. She was talking to a gentlemen and the other person seemed to be his wife, there was a touch of royalty in them, they stood there, to let her finish with her clients.

"Clients?" He asked Aria. "Yes dear, clients, they approached her to buy some of her paintings, but she doesn't believe in selling art, but to let them rest at unknown places, all hidden, or taste dirt after some days or months."

Strangely and curiously, he looked at the lady again, and then at Aria. "Oh...I got it," said Arav. "No...you don't, she is so complex to know," Aria smiled at him, "They are the clients who own the cinema hall in central and want to place her work there. She might agree with them, but not with the pieces they are asking for, I am sure, but one or two of the others only."

On completing her engagement with her clients, to which Arav was listening closely, she turned to her left, knowing that someone was waiting for her. "Aria," contentedly she called out her name, to which Aria responded, "Hey darling…I am seeing you now for the first time this evening...where have you been, busy ass?"

Arav had accidentally dropped his phone when the artist turned towards them, he bent down for his phone and while straightening back up, he looked at her, totally astounded by the very first look of her. "Whaaaat…?" he screamed within, it was Nasia, "What...Nasia is the artist? Am...am I dreaming again...if I am, wake the fuck up, you asshole," he couldn't let his words out, they rang thunderously inside.

"Nasia...someone wants to meet you, or rather, I want the both of you to meet," Aria said.

She then looked at him, "Arav, she is the one, the artist of the painting, Nasia." On hearing Aria, Nasia got a bit dazed, leaned towards her left and looked at Arav. Their eyes met again, full of questions and passion this time.

"Nasia…hey, I know her," he said to Aria. "Nasia," he called her name again, "You are the artist of the painting, and wait, you are an artist?" he asked her, astonished. "Why didn't you tell me when you met me there? You simply walked away after the call."

Aria was totally confused, but happy at the same time on coming to know that they both knew each other, already. "Guys, you know each other?"

"Yes we do," Nasia said to Aria with a calm smile.

"Haha…see, I told you, she is so complex to understand, right?" Aria turned to Arav. He simply stood there, totally confused on how to react, but happy to know that she was an artist. Aria laughed at the situation.

"I didn't want to tell you, sorry," she said compassionately, "I wanted to see your reaction, and know your thoughts on the piece, and I must say, that...that you have discerned the piece exactly as I wanted it to be discerned, and I haven't heard any understanding of it as beautifully expressed as yours.

"Aye...Nasia, he is a writer, of course he would understand your dynamics...haha," Aria claimed while looking at both of us.

"A writer," she said in an unstable and surprised voice, with an excited undertone, "A writer, whoa, you didn't tell me about that either, did you?" Nasia said, sighing.

"Well...I didn't...the same way as you," he said shyly.

There was a moment of silence then, and the two of them looked at each other quietly, while Aria felt like she was third wheeling, but being a good friend of Nasia, she wasn't made to feel like one. "Ahh guys, I think I should go now...or I'll be late." "Yes...sure darling...your relatives are coming to meet you, I forgot all about it," Nasia said while still looking at Arav, and then towards Aria.

"Yeah...at least you remembered that, lol...I think I should go now...happy fair, dear. Message me once you reach home... we'll meet tomorrow," Aria says to Nasia and then turned to Arav, "I would like to be in contact with you too, make sure you both share contacts, I'll get yours through Nasia, I am leaving now, take care both of you," Aria said, giving Nasia a hug and waving at Arav, before leaving.

They talked a little about the fair after Aria left and about all the artists and writers they liked, they discovered a lot of common names between them, they carried a lot of similarity between them, both knew very different worlds while living in the same. It was obvious, they both knew how to create another world, to forget all the miseries, to live in all the laughter, one wrote it while the other painted, each in their own most appropriate way. But what was it that stopped Arav from creating things sometimes? He loved dark, hated light too, kept on telling himself that light existed, whereas darkness was just the absence of light, therefore, there was nothing like darkness, but still, he seemed to embrace the thing that wasn't really there. He knew the reality of colours, blossoms, but still chose to live in the melancholy of sheer darkness.

Somewhere, the thinking of Nasia was relatable for him. Well, not in the whole, but perhaps a part of it. The things she showed in her paintings, it needed a certain complexity to be able to release it on a sheet, and Aria had already indicated her to be that to Arav. He wanted to know her more, they were in the middle of a conversation, when Nasia said that she was hungry, and that there was a café nearby.

Arav told her that he was about to say the same, he wanted to know her more and she claimed to feel the same. She asked, "Should we leave now?"

"Yeah, we must," said Arav.

Walking out of the fair, talking intellectually about existentialism, it was clear that she had deep interest in philosophy like Arav. She, with her bug eyes, a new shine in them, and a winsome smile too, that was enough for one to lose one's consciousness to. They arrived at the café, entering to a pure smell of caffeine that he loved, she breathed in calmly, after her tiresome duty at the fair, a relief. They made an order of coffee and a pizza, along with burritos, and their seats at the window table.

"Well, the food is really good, thanks for this," said Arav.

"Yes, it is. I too came here just yesterday, I liked it too," somewhere while talking the whole way from the fair to the cafe and even back at the fair, Nasia tried to understand the inner scream, or the reality of Arav. She discerned him closely, call it an artist's way, the pure soul she had met like herself. He listened to her story about the experience she had while learning music, it was all comedy, and then the time came when she did something that left him with no thoughts. She took a clip out of her purse, put it between her lips and teeth, made a bun with her hair, and then used the clips to hold it in place. Again, he saw that black spot on her neck.

"I don't want to catch you off-guard with this, but I am so forthright that way," he looked at her again, "But you look like a muse when you do things with your hair, and now the bun, I am gone, I guess," he said it all, not being able to keep it, despite knowing that they both were not all that familiar with each other yet, he said it anyway.

"Oh...oh...thank you, Arav...haha," she laughed, partly covering her face, yes, she blushed at the compliment. She was beginning to know the type of person he was and she liked him for it, "You are sweet, Arav...really."

"Oh I am not that sweet...haha," he said embarrassed. After finishing their food, he asked, "Would you like to come with me to this shop nearby, I need to buy a pen and a handmade diary."

"Sure, why would I mind, dear?" She looked at him and asked, "Have you been here before?" He responded, "No... no, I just met someone on my way to the fair, who has a shop here. I thought I might find something apt."

They pay the bill and look at each other, smiling, her pink lips, and his eyes seem bigger while they sew each other up close like that, what it must feel like for the sky, when the stars make their presence. We always desire the stars, to touch them, feel them, but wait, are you sure? Do you even know that the sky is not high; it is deep, deeper than you think it would be. Would you still desire them, if the sky becomes your ground? In the day it may seem mesmerising, but when night arrives, you will feel the fear of falling. The same sky you wanted to fly in will become the sky you'll fear of falling into the depths of. It is same with our inner self, we see how thunderous our inner self is, we see the world, we don't feel it, we can hear only the inner self, not realising it to be felt.

"Perceive yourself first, before questioning the milieu."

It had been a while since they started walking, following the directions that the utility shop owner had given Arav, when Nasia politely asked where it was, Arav said that it was suppose to be right there as they had been on the right path, as told by the man he had met in the tube.

Nasia looked to her right, where there was a stranded building, which seemed fit for the set of a horror film. She got bit compos mentis with the vibe of the place, while he browsed the maps for the utility shop nearby. "Are you sure, Arav? 'Cause it doesn't look like a place where we might want to stay at." This time she looks at the building's opposite side and read the board.

"What the fuck...are you kidding me?" he screams, "A cemetery?" He looks at Nasia, "A cemetery? Whaaat? He told me it's right here...not a cemetery... a shop, haven't we walked straight down the path?" He lost his mind.

Nasia fretted over Arav, trying to decipher him, looking at him and listening to his screams, she knew that there was something with him, he was not stable in the condition he was in at that moment.

"Arav...Arav...wait...look!" She held his hand and tried

to call him back, "Nothing's wrong, let's leave." She didn't mention the place again as she felt it malapropos to say anything.

"No, how could it be, answer me? I am alright, okay? It just can't be this way. I met the person in the tube and he was the one to tell me the directions to the fair and then to his shop, but what is this? Am I going through it again? Yes, I must be suffering from the shit again. Nasia, Nasia, look at me, do you think I am a fool? Well, I am not, believe me, help me, hear me, feel me, please. But why a cemetery, even if it was another one of my day-mares, why a cemetery still? To tell of my dole? The reality of life? Where people come to see their loved ones for the last time? But I have none, or maybe some, but why my end? I met the old man too, he said it would be alright, giving and describing to me the will of the feather." The thing worrying him the most was how he knew that there was something, a cemetery, or his subconscious mind, that made him totally lose his senses. Arav felt so bewildered and dismayed on coming to know that he was at a cemetery, instead of the freaking shop.

She could feel him; decoding him with her naked eyes. Nasia took a hold on him, stronger this time, held his face, hit his chest, contemplated him with her beauteous eyes, clasped a breath with her lips, partly whispering, "You are with me, Arav, look at me, look in my eyes, don't mislay your sight over me. Close your eyes, listen to my voice, darling. You are alright, I am here with you." He closed his eyes and tried to calm down, sweating.

"Here you lost, again, my dear,
cleave to me, let go all your fear,

dream dreams you,
let me turn the blue into a new hue,
for I am here,
sent, to be with the pure,
may the love and light to you,
you are your own lovely cure,
Amen, Amen"

Plash of her babbling voice in a whoosh, yet a muse of the gypsy angels, she said it by letting every word land down on him. She asked him to open his eyes after she finished, still holding his face, lighter this time, staring into his eyes, red. He was calm now, he wanted to scream but that urge ended somewhere in the world of Nasia's words. "Let go of your thoughts and we must leave from here too, come," she held his hand and turned around, leading him to the tube.

She knew then, she understood him, a bit. A lady who had only met him for the second time and talked to him for the first, knew how to deal with Arav. Nasia had been serene at the time he was panicking, she han't stopped him, she let him scream instead, but soon, she shut his mouth, to let the scream that was left to die there unsaid. Sometimes it works this way, to scream and to let the scream that is left to just die there, unsaid, to not let it live, she had done the same with him, calmly.

Arav came back to his senses, and on realising what he had just done due to his panic attack, he apologises to Nasia, feeling debased. He then looked at her hand holding his, griping tight enough to make him follow her. He stopped. "I know what you must be thinking right now, that I am crazy."

She turned to him and he continued, explaining himself, "I am not, I just got pa-" she stopped him from saying anything further.

"You don't need to say anything, I can feel your pain, Arav. It's alright, we are humans, right? Let's not talk about this, boy. Don't think too much about it," she made him understand. Nasia knew how to tackle the situation of a panic attack, but how? How did she calm him down so subtly? Perhaps it was her inherent artistic bend of philosophy, and her natural state of being which allowed her to be like that.

They took the tube back to London bridge. Sitting beside him, Nasia said, "You are so pure, dear. I am glad that we ran into each other today, and I owe Aria for the meeting, again."

He thought about their special meeting and said, "I don't know if it's true enough to believe or not, but thank you for what you did for me, I owe you."

"You owe me some good, good coffee by your hand.. haha."

"Yes sure, thanks again," he said with a smile of pain and happiness. They shared their contacts, and upon reaching the station, they departed for their respective homes; Nasia lived near Bank. While sharing some parting words before leaving, she expressed her concern for him. "I can reach home securely, thanks for the concern, believe me, I'll send you a message for sure," said Arav as they hugged and departed.

It was late in evening now. He left for his home after sharing a goodbye with Nasia and thanking her again for having spent the day with him. Ruminating over the day, he made a futile attempt to not think about how beautiful Nasia was, both inside and out, that got him so bad. Maybe, maybe he was falling. He messaged her upon reaching home safely, and she replied within a second, "Great, I just reached too. Whatever it is, whatever the time, just give me call, well, you are stronger than me anyway."

That pleased him. He did't want to eat anything for dinner, so after getting refreshed, he went straight to bed, thinking whether he would get any sleep or not, as today was a lot for him to take. He then messaged Anvisha to tell her to meet him soon.

Every morning will show you to you, every night shows the time to happen in coming present, belief plays with faith, grip it, to lose it is to lose yourself. Nothingness in time is the role-playing of the inner self, or to crave the foregone thoughts of being multi-personality within, entangled and tied to think about what are you thinking.

Chapter Four

Time being the biggest lie we keep telling ourselves, what if we don't apportion our time in the first place? The time that's gone never comes back, time is precious, time is everything, time decides, because we let it go on. They say, the time that has passed will never come back, but what about the memories we live from the past, hundreds of times. Like the rain we let fall from above, we let ourselves drown in the ocean of time - term insisted memory exists.

In the unmeasured depth of the sea, there lie untold stories...stories that have been seen and told by shipwrecks. They soon get swallowed down by the sea, to embrace the tears that have been bleeding the names of their beloveds, a sombre shadow of pain, untold, like the darkness of night, let there be no light. To feel the sheer silence is sometimes the way out for the scream that has long been held inside. We are always told to find the solution to our problems instead of sitting there alone, but have we ever been told to find the reason behind the problem, rather than its solution straight away? Deep down, we all know the truth, but fear to express it, fear to feel too, and fear to interact with...stand eye to eye in front of the mirror, fall free into our own depths, know ourselves, let our unspoken will tell us a new saga for it has been kept inside for so long, that it is longing to be told, to be felt, to be touched, to be seen, and not to be walked upon.

Every time, every single moment, the river of questions comes up to destruct you, don't fear it, but confront it... confront it with the strength that lives in you, for through a wan time like this, wait for them to be answered, 'cause they are not just questions, but your innocence, which is as meek as a dear, as weak as your fear, don't be loud, stay in silence to make it feel your absence, let the silence scream for you, let the dark search for you, let the light talk to live in you, and all the pain and sorrows laugh to be dead.

At some or the other time in our lives, all of us have felt that stage of sheer pain, and that scream within ourselves, unheard by others, even when you have vented it out in the best possible way available at that time being, being... the question of being, let it amaze you at every stage of your life, live with it, ask yourself if you really exist, but don't dive into it, it might be imperative but still is, at the end, useless.

Know the language of life, that is everything, and the mess that dreams are, write them down word by word, everything about the mess, and life, and dreams. For we all live in dreams, we see what we seek, and that seeks us with every breath we take, in the open air of imagination, as temporary and delicate as a mirror, that can't be stopped to be broken into pieces upon being hit with the harsh reality. It doesn't really care whom you came with, if it wants to happen to you, it will, there's no stopping it. It may perhaps stop if you start seeking the truth, what you have been running from, and fall in the trap created by time, dream, and life. After all, they all work together to tell you that you are small, but no... if you have indeed been small, why did they happen to you at all? To stop you? Yes, you are a barrier in their progress; don't let them be yours, in your success.

Alone is just a term to make you feel it. Look at it, how alone it lives, always keeping its eyes on you for its own company. But it's your choice, whether you want to be used by it, or derive success out of everything.

Shivering in the cold flurry of air at midnight, he tried

to pull the blanket over him, but found nothing. With a blurry sight, he looked for it, slithered off the bed and gathered it back. The thing to note was, he was sleeping that night, but had somehow gotten disturbed by not finding his blanket on him. Sighing to himself and feeling a bit light in the mist of midnight, he drifted back into a calm but fitful sleep, knowing that his thoughts might come back to hit him hard anytime again. He tried to sleep again, lying and releasing a blissful breath, and closed his eyes, thinking that he should sleep to rest his mind bit. Soon however, the sky started screaming, thunderous outside, as if it was asking to be heard, to unveil a saga to be told. Carrying a rainbow of thunders in his mind, he woke up again, with an increased heart-rate this time, and glanced at the sky, the colours of it, brightening beneath; he sat up and looked closely, to observe what was really happening. It was at this point that the darkness started to frighten him, with the only language of communication it knew: thoughts.

With every breath he took, his chest started to feel heavy, he felt sparks in his head, sparks that might lead to fire, at the stroke of an instant, he felt surrounded by laughter, with illusionary faces of unknown persons, not with actual human figures, but just figures of laugh art, he didn't know how to decipher it. Arav turned the lights on and making his mind blank again, went off to sleep, 'cause he knew that it was all just his illusion that was trying to grip him, but he wasn't going to let it happen.

His phone fell from the table, vibrating, Arav woke up and reached for it. The call was from an unknown number, he didn't want to sound sleepy, so he waited to regain full consciousness to be able to talk, then got up and answered the call.

"Hey, am I talking to Arav?" Asked an unfamiliar male voice, soft and mature.

"Hi, yes. And you are?" he responded with a questioning tone.

"Yeah, I am calling from the Muse of Words, the competition. This is with regard to the submission you sent for the journals. Congratulations! You made it. We will be publishing your poetry. Kindly check your e-mail, you need to submit a fee for it. We have sent the rest of the details there, sir, congratulations once again." It had caught Arav so off-guard and he got so surprised, that he didn't even know how to react, having woken up to this phone call, he wanted to scream with happiness.

"Whoa, I didn't expected that! Thank you, sir. Yes, I'll take care of the rest of the formalities, thank you," he said in excitement.

"Sir, the pleasure is ours, take care," he said and the line went dead.

What had happened over the previous night didn't amaze him the way this morning did. He wanted to tell Anvisha about it as soon as possible. He made a call to her, it kept ringing, but she didn't answer. Perhaps she was sleeping, or was in the shower. He thought of calling Nasia to tell her about the news, but was faced with a dilemma of whether he should call her immediately, or after an hour, as it was only 10:30 in the morning then. He freshen up, singing, made himself breakfast and coffee, and without calling his landlords, went straight up to them, for he had promised to meet them, to surprise the beautiful couple. On his way to their house, which was hardly 8 to 10 minutes of walk from his apartment, he bought some roses from a street vendor.

He rang the bell, Mrs. Walsh opened the door and found him outside on his knees, offering her white roses. She was so surprised and happy on seeing him, as he had arrived all of a sudden, and while accepting the flowers from him, she hugged him, saying, "Oh, dear, how we missed you! Welcome, come inside," with a big calm smile on her face. He entered their house and found uncle James sitting and watching television while having his chocolates. He turned around, looked at Arav and immediately got up to meet him with a renewed charm and glow on his face. He offered the flowers to uncle too, which brought a great beautiful smile on his face and he laughed. "Oh, boy, thank you for this, haha... how have you been?We missed your visit, young man," he said in his calm and soothing old man's voice. "I missed you both too. I've been great, sir, how have you been?" he said, hugging him.

"Haha…both of us have been great, look at our faces now. Come sit," he said happily and after a short pause, asked his wife, "Dear, would you mind giving him some coffee?"

"Oh, lord…haha, why would I mind? I'll get one for you, Arav, and one for myself...haha...your uncle missed you, he has stories to tell you, I can't listen to them now, I am tired… haha."

Arav couldn't say no to whatever they said, for he owed them big time. While she got coffee for Arav and herself, he got busy with uncle James in a conversation about some series, in which a young lad murders her beloved and then kill himself for having committed the sin by committing another. He didn't know about the series, nothing, but he listened to it intently as uncle James was so excited to talk to the man he liked the most, perhaps. Mrs. Walsh came to sit next to Arav too, they shared laughter, talked about his life for a while and his poetry submission that had just gotten accepted. They were so happy to hear it, as if they belonged to to him only. In the middle of their conversation, they heard the bell ring, they had a visitor.

"Ah, it must be Shelly," the aunt said. Arav looked curiously at her, being unfamiliar with the name. When she noticed, she said, "Shelly is my sister, Arav. She needs me to go with her for something related to her work at the pottery farm...I'll be right back."

"It was such a pleasure to meet you, dear. Please keeps visiting us, I'll try to be back soon. If I don't, come to meet me again sometime, I'll be waiting." She kissed his cheek and got up to get the door. After Shelly exchanges some pleasantries with uncle James and Arav, they depart.

It was so calm and quiet at their house, it soothed him a lot. The place was not too crowded either, except when they had children over, then the house would reverberate with their laughter and play.

Uncle James was closely observant of people, and while talking to Arav, he observed his behaviour. He was happy, but not heartedly. He didn't say a word about it to Arav, as he didn't want to make him feel uncomfortable or worried. Instead, he told him a story of a sluggish guy, who always blamed God for everything. When things went well for him, he claimed to be an atheist, but when bad things went down, he accounted it all to God's will.

"Young man, I have something for you. I have been holding it for many days to tell you, and now that you are here, you ought to listen to it," he said in his soothing voice, looking at the ceiling.

"Oh...sure uncle, your stories, yeah, it's always a pleasure to listen to them, you always make me live through your stories. Please." He wanted to hear it, he liked his stories and the way he narrated them, most of which were his own experiences, or those witnessed by him. Uncle James proceeded.

"There are some people who, despite knowing everything, the outcome of their decisions, commit mistakes. But a mistake done more than twice is not a mistake anymore, it becomes a habit. I don't know why people don't understand that both joy and sorrow hold equal emotional significance in a human's life." He paused for a moment and took a sip from his glass of wine.

"Neil liked to wait, determined by hope, for the good to come, instead of learning the language of reason. He waited instead of looking for answers. He asked for the labyrinths of the pit of joy, a maze of joy he asked every moment, instead of the goddamn sky of it...not knowing the root of his mishaps, he always cut the branches, knowing that the branches are always weaker than the whole tree.

Stepping into the world of nihilism, he found it easy to question the useless, saying that his soul is a bottomless pit of pain and despair. What he didn't know, Arav, was that a soul could also be a bottomless reservoir of joy and love and care, if only he had let it be, but he never did, so why would he have felt great about it, anyway?" Arav was no longer with uncle James then, he was there physically in front of him, but in his mind, he was lost in his words, trying to experience what uncle James had been saying.

Uncle James looked around and rested his gaze at the mirror. "Look there, if the mirror, that completes you by showing you the thing you want to see, breaks...breaks into pieces, it'll reflect the complete you in those pieces, shattered and separated. Would you then wait for it to stick back together to make a whole mirror again, or ask God, the power unseen, or would you hope for it? Let me tell you what you should actually do, you should work for it." He paused.

"Work, uncle? I didn't get it." He was left in questions.

"Yes, boy. Your hopes, prayers and waiting won't do any help, would they? Oh well, they might have, had you been living in the Kingdom of Frozen or the Wonderland of Alice, but in the real world, nothing but working for it will do. To make those pieces stick together and make a whole mirror out of it will cut your fingers, the sharp edges or the very tiny pieces, and it will never become the mirror that it used to be, there would indeed be some gaps, but you need to do it nonetheless. It's not in the pieces that you're reduced to hail a glow of yourself, if you know what I mean. You don't have to be that guy." Uncle James stopped, staring into his eyes, which reflected his unstable inner self.

"Who was Neil in the story, Uncle? How do you know that guy?" Arav asked curiously.

"Neil could be anyone. Go outside, look around, you'll see many of him in the world," he said, drowning in the last sip of his wine.

New thoughts started embracing him, he felt their whisper and their touch. What he had heard from Uncle James, was not just a story, but a lesson, and he had known exactly how to teach that lesson. On coming to know the answer to the guy's dilemma, the first person he could think of was none other than himself. He closed his eyes and told himself that the cuts he would risk trying were better than sitting in the corner, head down, and waiting…for absolutely nothing. He thanked uncle James for the lesson he had just taught him. He replied, "My pleasure, young man. I am glad that you heard the very idea closely and have accepted it. Stay blessed."

He realised that he had spent quiet a long time at their house and had to leave, in order to talk to Nasia and Anvisha and tell them all about the day's happenings. He asked for uncle James' permission to leave, as a gesture of respect. Departing, he said, "I'll visit you again soon. Thank you and stay blessed, uncle James. It's always a pleasure to come by, and please tell aunt that I had to leave."

"You can come by anytime you want, consider us as your own. Don't be stressed about anything, just come over. And yeah...I'll tell your aunt. Oh...these ladies are never on time.. haha."

After giving uncle James a final hug, he left, tangled in the essence of entangling. Here was a lesson, a pure dose of reality and life, which he wanted to share with Nasia immediately, but he made his way back home first, getting himself something to eat on the way. He checked into his mail and completed the formalities and fee submission for his selected poem. He then called Nasia. She picked up at the third ring. "Hi Arav, how are you?" she answered the call, before letting him say anything first.

"Hey Nasia, I am great, what about you? You are always so quick and excited," he said, a bit nervous and excited himself.

"Haha...yeah, I am good too. I know...I know, that's my other art, haha...what're you up to?"

"Haha, yeah I wanted to tell you about something, and it's beautiful."

"What is it...tell fast." She couldn't wait to hear it, the same way as he couldn't wait to tell her.

"Some days ago, I sent a submission for a poetry journal in the Muse of Words, and this morning I got a call from them, telling me that they have accepted my submission. They'll be publishing it very soon," he finally told her.

Nasia mirrored his excitement on the other end of the line. "What…are you serious?…I mean, it's...it's just wow, you made it, amazing, I am so happy, oh God." She felt so ecstatic upon hearing the news, as if it was her own poetry that had gotten accepted. Arav could hear someone else with her too, who was shouting excitedly with Nasia.

"Thank you, Nasia. Are you with somebody? Did I disturbed you?"

"Aye, it's Aria. We had planned to meet today. She is so excited for you too, Arav." Her tone became more subtle, second by second. "Where are you? Can we meet by any chance?"

"Oh...say my hello and thanks to Aria. Yeah sure, I am up-to nothing, really, where are you?

"We will be at Convent Garden in 10, meet us there?"

"Convent garden, okay sure. See you there in 30," Arav said and cut the call.

Hearing her voice, there was something that placed him in a state of tranquil, he could feel her words, that were gone now, but were still in his ears, shivering down to his heart. He knew already that he might fall for the beauty kept inside for so long and for the one who really did unravel him, at the very first meeting. He, for a while, felt alive, the journal and her voice, he now knew what to do next, but it was not him, it was his inner self that urged him to write for Nasia. But he wouldn't now, in a piece of sheer nature, he would write of her beauty. Arav got ready to meet her and Aria, left home ten-minutes after the call, took a bus, not the tube, for he wanted to hail the sky. On getting there, he looked around for them, made a call to Nasia again, but she didn't pick up this time. "Her phone might be on silent mode," he said to himself. After a while, he made a call to her again, but she didn't pick up this time either. He wondered why she would do that, when she herself had asked him to meet her. He had no thoughts running in his mind, all he thought about was her. Hopelessly, he kept his phone back in his pocket and did nothing besides standing there, blank, looking at the sky; some birds flying in a V-formation calmed him. At that moment, someone approached him from behind and covered his eyes with their palms. Arav trembled with fear for a moment, but on feeling the touch, the touch which lived in him, he realised that it was the same touch, that had caught him. "Umm hmm, tell my name?" A voice whispered and the words murmured.

"Oh...should I call you a light of night, or a desired destruction?" he said casually.

She didn't know what he was saying, and the smile on her face started turning into one of curiosity.

"Maybe a canvas of joy, or a painted blue sky?"

"Then...lady, I would like to call you Nasia," he said with a slight laughter.

She pulled back her hands, looked at him with a smile of want, and wondered at the meaning of his words. She knew what it was, but she reacted as casually as Arav had said the words. Aria stood there with lines on her forehead, trying to understand what it was, but whatever it was, she was happy for them. She knew that they were perfect to be together, but she didn't say anything as she wanted it to unfold with the flow, not interrupting the sequence that God had made. Nasia and Arav met, shared a smile, hugged, and then he looked at Aria, who had been standing to his left. They didn't share any word at that moment, their eyes said enough.

"I think I exist too. O'lord, where am I?" Aria said, looking towards the sky and extended her arms upwards.

Arav looked to his left, while Nasia was lost somewhere. "Oh... a lady asking for pity," he said, "Haha...sorry, Aria... how are you, dear?"

"I think I am great alone," Aria laughed dramatically. "I am great. Congrats, Arav. Nasia told me about the poetry thing. Now, I think I should make friends with these birds. At least they'll look at me and acknowledge that I exist too," she cocked her head to one side and continued saying dramatically.

"Aria, stop," said Nasia, "Haha...oh you girl, haha...stop." Aria and Arav hugged, talked about the fair where they had first met, and how they were here again. "I want something to eat, shall we?" Aria asked.

They laughed and Arav repeated the same thing, "I am always hungry, let's go." They went for some street food in that perfect weather of the day, a day of calmness. While Aria ate her hot dog and Nasia her waffles, a thought suddenly stroke him, a thought of Anvisha. "Agh...I forgot to call her."

"Who?" Nasia asked.

"There's this friend of mine, from childhood, she didn't pick my call this morning, I had to tell her about the journals," he said, making a call to Anvisha again. "Oh...sure, I would like to meet her someday," Nasia said, while Aria was still having her hot dog, eating as if she hadn't eaten for days. Anvisha picked up this time.

"Where have you been, Anvisha? I had to tell you something, what are you doing?" he asked, a bit relieved on hearing her voice. "Sorry, I forgot. Yeah, what is it?" she asked.

"I made it to the journals. They accepted my submission and will be publishing it soon."

"What? That is amazing Arav, great work! I am so happy for you, beautiful," she said with a subtle, yet happy tone.

"Yeah thanks, and there's one more thing," he took a pause for her to respond. "What is it?" she asked. "There's someone I would like you to meet. Her name is Nasia, I met her at the art fair." She, Nasia, smiled at him, while nodding a 'yes'.

Anvisha didn't say anything. She continued to listen to Arav, whatever he had been saying about the journals, about Nasia and Aria, and responded with a slight crack in her voice, "Oh...great...I...I would surely like to meet, soon, I...I got to do some work now, sorry, and congrats, we'll meet soon."

He observed something inapt in Anvisha's reaction to his words, he didn't say much but remarked that she was in the middle of something. Nasia was looking at him, and wondered what was wrong. She kept it to herself, but noticed a certain curiosity in him. The three of them spent the evening together, went to places nearby, listened to buskers, shared their thoughts and some experiences. The way he looked at Nasia, was the way of galaxy to be told, and Aria noticed it all. Somewhere, the artist knew about it too, but she kept quiet. Arav told both of them about his wonder and gratitude, saying, “When we met, you got me so well, Nasia. It’s all because of this beautiful lady, Aria. It’s only after I met you two, that I got selected. I feel relieved and I slept well at night. Thank you for happening to me, both of you.” He stopped and broke his eye-contact with them to avoid embarrassment.

“Yeah,” Aria said, “It’s just been a day, but I think we’d go very far together. The vibes you share are so positive, writer.” Nasia, meeting his silence by her own silence, said, “Yeah, we had to meet, I guess. Whatever it is, it is beautiful and it must stay, forever.

He knew that he had something to write on her or for her. Nasia and Aria got busy talking about something related to their relatives, who knew each other, while he was lost in thoughts about writing a trail of an ocean, thinking about ideas, when Nasia interrupted his thoughts and asked him about Anvisha. She asked him to tell them something about her. When they reached a cafe, she said, “You said you two have been together since childhood. What is she like? I mean, by nature and all. I am sure she must be great though, if you have been with her, but still, tell me something about her, if you want to.” Of course, she must be excited to know his friend, when they have this close, after that disgust night, of Arav.

“Ahh...well, she is beautiful and very polite, caring and understanding. She knows exactly what I want, each time.” He stammered with his words a little, thinking a lot before saying anything about her. He got caught, as if he was hiding something. Aria didn’t catch it, but the dynamic Nasia deciphered it, while listening to him and noticing his gaps in words, closely.

While he sipped his coffee, Nasia took a hold of his hand and said, "You said you slept well last night, didn't you? Tell me what was that about?" For a moment, he had no words to let out. He was shocked and wondered why she asked him that in the first place. "Well yeah, I did. (He took a pause to think whether he should tell her or not.) I woke up at midnight to collect my blanket that had slid off the bed, It was thundering out, which had disturbed my sleep. Rest, I slept quite well." Nasia frowned at his words and said, "Arav...thundering? when? The weather was absolutely clear last night. I know it because I was onto something and slept at two. Besides, if there had been any thunder, I would have woken up, my sleep is usually not very deep." Aria was sitting right next to them and was listening without saying a word. She knew that it would become quite awkward if she indulged with them. Arav frowned at Nasia, hoping for her to reveal that it was all a joke and that she had been lying. 'How could it be?' he wondered. All his thoughts starting co-occurring, and Nasia was totally aware of that. This time, she let his inner self come out, his foregone thoughts too, the thoughts of having been friends with someone, or if he existed himself, the people he knew, the cemetery and the sleepless nights, and now this. "It can't be true, maybe...maybe it came all of a sudden when you had slept, or perhaps…it was only in my area, right…that's it, I know." He stole his gaze from them and looked into his coffee, which had now turned cold. He gulped it all down at once. She knew that he was not alright. She had known it since the very start when she first met him at the fair, and now she knew that something was wrong with regard to Anvisha.

"Arav...Arav, it's alright. Sometimes, when there's too much work load or something that is bothering you, it creates certain images in your head to think that way. The same happened with Aria two days back. She experienced the same thing, as she was under a lot of pressure due to her work, and it was all about the art that she saw in her room." Aria was stunned to hear these words, she left her coffee and stared at Nasia, all blank. She didn't know what to say, or understand why Nasia was dragging her into this discussion by giving an example that never took place, ever. But Nasia knew what she was doing. Arav looked at Aria and asked her if she was alright now. She didn't know how to react. "Oh... yeah, it just happens sometimes, you know," she said with an embarrassed smile, while still feeling blank and confused. She turned to Nasia with a questioning look.

He knew, however, that Aria never went through anything like this, but didn't say anything about it. He told Nasia that he would be alright. "The thunders might point to my inner self right now, which is not stable, but it will be. You will do it." Without giving him a break to think anything else, or to reveal anymore of his thoughts, Nasia said, "Well, forget it. Let's spend a good time." Aria was so confused, but she knew that Nasia's complexity was the best thing that could help, especially an artist like her, as she herself couldn't understand her totally. "Arav...do you mind showing me Anvisha's picture, please? Because I am so excited, I want to meet your friend. I don't know why, it's just that I want to know you more." Arav, breathing heavily, wondered what it might be? Whenever she asked about her, what happened to him? He confusedly looked at her and Aria, who were waiting for his response.

"Uhh, I might not have a picture of her," he thought about it again, "Yeah, I don't." They were dismayed to hear that. "What? Arav...she is your childhood friend, and you don't have even a single picture of her? Don't joke, and show it to us."

But what he had said was true, he didn't have a single picture of her, or with her. He cogitated about it again, should he tell them the truth about Anvisha, or was it not the appropriate time to let them know? "What, Arav, we are waiting, you know it too, it can't be possible to not have a single memory that close a mate of yours, or is it that you don't want us to see her?" Nasia remarked, in a more serious tone this time. He was left with no choice, he had to tell them. "If not pictures, isn't she on any social media? It's not possible that she is not. If she exist, she must be," Aria said.

Being sentient and trying to lighten his chest to get things out and share with the right people, he said, "Okay, to be honest, Aria, she is not on any social media site, nor do I have a picture of her with me. I know, I know, it must sound so crazy, but that's true." Nasia tried to say something, but her words didn't come out. He read her expression and said, "Listen Nasia, listen, okay, well...Anvisha does not socialised. It's her mental health that she is suffering from. She fears crowds and meeting people, feels cramped if she sees her own picture, and doesn't allow anyone to take it too. She never shows up on video call, not even with me. It's not that I didn't want to tell you, but it's true." Both of them were in great distress to come to know this. Aria held her head down, as if she was getting a bugbear in her head, while Nasia didn't know how to respond. "Wait, do you mean to say that she is suffering from Acrophobia?" she asked in a rustling voice.

"No, not really Acrophobia. She can go out, acrophobic fear to even go out. She doesn't meet people though. I think she is somewhere in the Acrophobic spectrum, that I don't know. She came back to London only recently from her hometown, to work."

"Oh...hmm, okay, to work? Where?" Nasia asked.

"Oh, I never really asked. Because she thinks that if I know, I'll keep an eye on her. I don't know why, but yeah, she does. She once told me that it's a publishing house, where she had to proofread something, but where and what the name of the place is, I don't know."

Arav finally let it out. Somewhere in him, he didn't want to accept it, it was a sorrow for him, and the joy that had no laughter at times. He knew it, but he couldn't help her, he want to, but couldn't. Nasia asked him to let her meet Anvisha to help her out, and he knew that she could understand anyone, in a great way too. But he himself feared to let her meet Anvisha, but why? What was left for him to tell? Nasia could smell his fear that was burning beneath. There was something else that had to be vent out. "It's okay, just let me know whenever we can meet."

"Sure," he said.

She has a feeling for Arav, she could guess that he was going though something mighty, but didn't want to accept it himself. They were growing closer, hour by hour, it was strange that they had just met some time ago, but what will be, will be, that's the thing they knew.

It was 3:30 in the afternoon and he was feeling tired, maybe because the previous night's sleep had not been enough for him, and Nasia could clearly see that. "Arav, I guess you should get some rest, dear," she said, as she felt it would be the best for him at that moment. "Yeah, I need some rest, I guess." Before leaving for the bus, he asked Nasia and Aria out for a dinner the next day. Well, it was not strange, but quiet quick, however, it didn't matter. "Oh sure,

Arav. I am glad you asked, no issues. We'll come for it," Nasia said, but there was something that was bothering Aria. She said, "I guess you both should go, I don't want to third-wheel your date anymore."

"A date, haha," he laughed. "Yeah, it's a date you fool, haha," Aria replied. "I think we should go together some other time. Get together soon, you both," she said.

"Well, haha, as you say, Aria. I respect that too, haha."

"Well, I know, I am cool," Aria guffawed.

Arav was excited for it, so was Nasia. She told him where she wanted to go, for he had asked her for the place of her choice. Nasia told him of a place that would be perfect at night for their 'date'. "It's a calm place to be. We'll meet at Tower Bridge at 8, would 8 be great?" she asked. "Oh, yeah sure, that's great, haha, but what's the name of the restaurant?" he asked. She didn't tell him the name, for she wanted to keep it a surprise. Within ten-minutes after that, he left for his home, so did they.

On his way back, he knew what to do: write for her. If she could give him a surprise for the date, then he should reveal his poetry to her too. A few lines for her, he decided to pen them down the same day, for he had a lot of things going on in his mind.

There was a kind of rush in him, that kept Nasia, her words and her voice (oh! what a voice it was!) alive in his memory. She was a muse, his muse, and his therapy. He wanted to hold her hand, hold her tight, but he didn't for the sake of his senses and emotional control. He knew, however, that he would say it all the next day, at their dinner table. He would say what he felt for her, it was surely a quick move, but for him and an unravelling lady like her, it would be a perfect moment. Maybe, like a fairy story of an interrupted guy like Arav and entangled lady like Nasia.

He changed his clothes, thinking of Nasia and the richness of her words that were still echoing in his mind. After long, he turned the television on, just as a background sound, and lay on the bed, looking at the ceiling. After a moment, he turned to his left to see what was on the television, a random comedy show. He thought of everything that he could write for Nasia, closed his eyes, took a pen and a diary, and started writing. But the condition of the pages was not as serene as his feelings at all. There were so many revisions, scratching and free-handing, but after a while, he came up with something much better, and started anew on the next page. It was not with great length, but with depth that his words came into being.

In the time of my era,
the saga, I won't
and blood beseeched,
dripped over your eyes, my throat.

Then the fairy, fairs,
occurs to me,
holding her sun to bright my moon,
clashing the waves to be.

In the mist, we are bound,
for to love, love,

would I be destruct,

by the precious dove, O'dove.

After writing these lines, he folded a paper, on which something was written. Then, he tore the page with these words out of his diary and put it in a small book, that he was going to give to her. The paper which he had folded before, which he had already torn apart, even before writing the above lines, might have had a full length of it, or perhaps he wrote the poetry, the introduction to which is above.

Chapter Five

Before he could even close his diary, he felt something vibrating, he looked for it under the pillow, it was his phone, ringing on silent mode. Anvisha was written on the screen. He got a bit suspicious by that. What must it be, he thought, as he greeted, "Hey."

"Hi," she replied with a pale voice. "Why did you do this Arav, I...I don't know how to riposte you."

He didn't know what she was talking about. In an instant before replying, he thought if he had done something to her, "What's wrong, dear? What have I done? Are you alright? What is it?"

She got all upset, her voice pale, he could imagine her growing white. Anvisha seemed to be on the verge of an outburst, as if he had betrayed her. "What's the matter? What have I done wrong? Are you seriously asking all this, despite knowing everything? Oh...since when have you started hiding things, Arav, since when?" Her pitch got higher word by word, her anger was so intense, a bold-wired bond of all electricity in a single piece.

"You told her everything, didn't you?" She sounded hurt. "Didn't you tell your new friend about this old mate, everything about this old friend's situation, didn't you?" She pauses for a moment to breathe, her voice had started to break. Before she could say anything further, Arav interrupted, "Wait, what? What you saying, dear? How would you know if told her or not?" He was trapped, but the thing that was worrying him the most was how had she come to know about it.

“Arav, I know it, the time you called me, she was with you, and must be thinking why I didn’t talk to her, right? You obviously would have told her everything, she sounded close to you, why Arav?”

“Listen, Anvisha, it’s not like what you taking it to be, yeah…I am sorry that I told her about you, but she understands, believe me, I had to tell her about you, if I hadn’t, I would have had to lie, everyday, you know it, I know...I know what you must be feeling right now, dear. I am really sorry, but it had to be done this way.” He stopped, got up from the bed, drank some water, then said, “You there?”

“Yeah, yeah I am, I am just really hurt, but I am glad that you told the truth to me and to her, but still Arav.” She was calm now, still a pain was there in her voice. “Someone knows your secret now.”

My secret, he thought to himself, mulling over why she had said that. ‘My secret, what must it mean? It was her secret, but maybe she meant that as being her friend, it was my responsibility to keep it too, hence, it had become mine too, but no...that was not her tone.’ He said, “Anvisha, my secret?”

“Ah, yeah, I mean, our secret, or mine,” she swallowed, “It’s okay, Arav. I will talk to you when I feel better, don’t call me, I’ll call you by myself, soon. Please, let me be alright a bit.” On hearing these words, he felt a bit of release, but he felt hurt too, at her condition then. He didn’t say much, as he knew her well. He could feel her, he knew she had meant what she said. “Okay, but please, do it soon, I’ll be waiting, and I am sorry again.” Saying goodbye and take care, she cut the call.

Everything felt a bit messed-up to him, but he soon felt an ease of release when he positioned his mind to the upcoming night, that he was going to be with Nasia, her memory was enough for him. It was at this moment that he came to realise that he had no picture with Nasia either, and made a mental note to take one that night. He conjectured if Nasia was with someone or not, but thought why she would have asked him to meet her, and then say yes to the date had there been someone else with her in the recent past.

Whispers of silence to find the foregone pieces of ourselves, and to come closer to us, is the best way for them to become a part of us. To know the deal in the way, the world smiles and to forget the misery and pain of yesterday, to be lost in the enrichment of tomorrow or beneath the realness in the world of smiling fakes being truthful to the dark, light shows its different colours that may change to complete the glow of the sky, to imprint the rainbow on your smile. Grey, we become, to pale the light in etiolating time, but to embrace the dark is to embrace your own falsity, to shine, we need a light to reflect on us, but how will dark reflect you, when it has no colour in it?

To him, it was not just a date. He was going to recite poetry that he had written for her. All he wanted to do at that time was to say it out loud, he didn't want to wait for later, but to let it go with the flow, to released the dammed water. Maybe, maybe she might bring the light he had been searching for within, but couldn't find it like a forgotten wall of joy that had vanished in the air with time. In the end, it's just the pain we remember that the world gave us, not the joy.

At 8, Nasia sent a message to him, just to remind him. It was 6:45 in the evening and he was reading a book. He got the very elevation as usual, taking a shower at noon before starting with reading, and the great thing was, he had slept the previous night, uninterrupted. He got up on seeing her message, reached for the closet, fighting with his thoughts and the very ideology of the text –Clarissa by Samuel Richardson, on the theme of an individual and the society.

Wearing a blackish trouser and a burgundy shirt, with black shoes, shinny yet matt, and taking the paper in his pocket, he left at 7:30, knowing that he would reach there by 8, exact. Taking a bus again, he hailed a new glow of joy, elevated with the thoughts of reciting poetry and for the place, as he didn't know what it would be. He made his presence there at 8, dot. Looking at the offices there, he sat near the river and waited for her, not making a call.

Within a moment, when he was sitting there, he looked at the river, listening to its beautiful sound, and feeling the breeze touch his face, he closed his eyes to feel the purity, while sitting there, not going over the river view. "Waiting for someone?" a familiar bonny voice asked. Arav looked over his back, there she was sitting. "Not really, just waiting to be approached by a spell-caster like you," he said while eyeing her down, spell bound. She smiled at him, but the thing he seascaped and the words she shared in her voice of a muse, yeah, he was numb.

She did not have a lot of make-up on, but the black shade lipstick, not yet black, and her eyes done with kohl, looked perfect. Her hair were undone, messy, yet entangled, and a dress of dark blue, plain, simple, eye-catching. He couldn't get his eyes off of her, as usual, when he saw her, he got all the way dumb and numb, but today was special too. "What? Could you please stop making me blush now, shall we go? she asked. "Oh yeah, haha, I can't help it, yeah come, take me."

Talking about the day, complimenting each other on their clothes, and the speciality of the day, an Artist with a Writer, amalgamated to be. She took him where she wanted to be on this night, she knew the brisk of the time, but maybe she wanted it, somewhere. A restaurant and a fine dine, but with a different aura, soothing. Lights were perfectly dim, it was an open restaurant, with candle light, covered subtly so the wind didn't blow them off, calm atmosphere, with light theme and soothing music, a very small stage, for karaoke, as there was a man, nearly of 40, singing songs, old with a modern touch, everything was perfect there, Nasia had a reservation near the stage and the view of Thames and the soothing buildings. He was happy to be at a place like this, he liked the vibes, and when he took his hand into his pocket to feel the paper, the same he was going to recite, it gave him some real chills.

Sitting at their table with pink candlelight, the fragrance of rose and jasmine at the same time, it was perfect for them. He looked around to glimpse at the positivity and others. Nasia called the waitress and said something to her, he didn't understand or hear anything that she said, as she had called her closer to speak. "What is it?" he asked. "Oh, it's nothing," she looked for someone with her calm eyes, and then back to him. She said after a pause, "Close your eyes, now." He looked at her questioningly; baffled, he closed his eyes and asked, "What? You are surprising me for the second time, haha, now what?" He didn't ask much, but just listened to her. "You can open them now, slowly," her voice sounded nearby and excited. He saw her standing and holding something, hiding behind her back.

He looked impatiently, wondering what it could be. "What? Haha, what is it, Nasia?" She held it with both her hands, offering him to take it with a winsome smile, in perfect time. It was a flower bouquet, small but beautiful, colourful, perfect scent, natural. He got pleasantly surprised by seeing that in her hands, he was happy and wanted to shout, but couldn't let his voice come out. She read his eyes, growing bigger and bigger every second, he looked at her, trying to say something, galvanised.

"It's okay, oh God...haha, you don't have to say anything, your eyes did," she said, extending the flowers to him to take a hold, he slowly grabbed it.

"Whoa, y...you didn't have to, but thank you, dear." He expressed his gratitude, excited that he was going to recite soon.

"I am glad that you liked it," she said. Sharing their joy; they talked about almost everything, from reincarnation philosophies to outer space. He got up, saying that he needed to go to the toilet, she nodded. She watched him walk away, smiling and blushing, flicked her hair back, the ones coming over her face, covering it. Arav went to toilet, and after coming out, called for the same waitress Nasia had called, and asked for a favour. He didn't want the stage but just the music to stop when he would ask for it, as he wanted to give her the surprise poetry. The waitress understood it, and asked him to just wave his hand at her whenever he wanted it to be, and added, "It is beautiful to see a couple like you guys, where your girl called for the bouquet surprise, and now you." He laughed a bit and told her that they were not a couple yet. "Oh, then you both will be for sure, stay blessed, just wave at me whenever you are ready." Thanking her, he headed towards his table, where she was sitting and still struggling to hold her hair back, as she didn't want to make a bun. "Had you slept in there?" she asked, as he had taken quite some time to come back from the toilet.

"Haha, nearly," he responded, embarrassed but excited.

Nasia had already ordered the food without even asking him, as she was quite sure that he would like what she had ordered, he had no issues with it, and knew that he was going to like it, as it would have taken millions of minutes to order food by himself. Her eyes were so shiny, like containing a galaxy in them, fair, Arav couldn't stop himself from stare into her eyes. "What? haha, you're making me shy," she said. He knew she would say this, and responded, "But your eyes are not". He thought that now was the time, when both were in the same romantic zone under the shining bright moonlight, which was reflecting upon her face so beautifully. He stood up, looked for the waitress, who got him and stopped the music in a moment. Nasia tried to decipher why he had stood up, not really thinking about the music. "What is it? Are you alright, Arav?" He smiled at her, took two steps closer to her, took out the piece of poetry and said, "Yeah, I may not be now." She didn't know what wass happening, she looked around, the waitress and the singing man looked at them, as if waiting for something. She turned back to him and said, "Arav, whaat?" gesturing through her hands, shrugging. He took a good beautiful long breath, exhaled and continued, "Nasia," he stopped for a moment, "It's for you, a piece of truth, I hope you like it, I know though, haha." Her mouth was left open, the couple sitting at the next table turned to them, he started.

In the time of my era,
the saga, I won't
and blood beseeched,
dripped over your eyes, my throat.

Then the fairy, fairs,
occurs to me,
holding her sun to bright my moon,
clashing the waves to be.

In the mist, we are bound,
for to love, love,
would I be destruct,
by the precious dove, O'dove.

He took a moment off, drank a glass of water, so happy, but nervous at the same time. The smile on her face was still constantly big, her eyes grew bigger, shrugging, shying, she looked around as everyone was looking at them, smiling. To avoid the embarrassment, she bit her lips and looked at the moon, the full-moon, and then back at him, as he said further:

Fair love, let us go dine,
Will thou let me call thee mine?
Will thou let me write fine?
Will thou let me taketh thee to a shrine?

For the sake of love, life, and liberty,
Will I be in your arms?
Will I be dirty?
With all your harmless harms?

If light wisian to dark,
Will thou be here to hark?
To ahreddan me from phantasm ark?
To become my matriarch?

For the sake of dead, dejected and despair,
Will I be in your walls?
Will I be out of my nightmare?
With all my flawless flaws?

O'beloved, bound me in your spell,
Taketh me out from hell,
Taketh me in your dell,
For in you, I've seen my bethel.

He breathed in the pure air, a deep breath, looked around as everyone applauded him, cheering him on, some even hooting. He looked at her, the made eye contact, her eyes were red, a drop of tear dropped over her face, then another, and another to her lips, she let fall, still, contemplating, sucked her lips, her cheeks were pinkish red, and then she covered her face with both hand, as if she was hiding from crying, maybe shrinking in her own, he took her. Grabbed her by her shoulder, kneeing on the floor, he said, "Nasia, look," he said in a lowered voice, "Hey, it was just what I felt for you, I wrote it down. Each and every word seemed so worthy to me, that I thought of venting it out to you, today itself, and I am glad I did. Hey, look." He let her take her moment, she hugged him so tight, lost in his arms, same with him, he kissed her forehead, calling her dear and dove. He said, "It's okay, let's eat, haha, I am hungry, or the food will go cold, yeah?" Nasia nodded, he went back to his seat. "Thank you, Arav," she said with a shivering voice. They had their food, he complimented her choice of food, and he really liked it. It was all good now.

They talked and talked, laughing at each other, till nothing was left on their lips while eating, or moustache while drinking. While indulging with him more and more, she tried to get into him. What she was worried about, was his relation with Anvisha, and she was trying to learn the complexity of it. After getting done with his food, he went to the toilet, this time for real, leaving his phone on the table. When Nasia lay her sight over the phone, she took a chance by taking it, despite knowing that it was a bad move. She unlocked it (he had told her the pass-code), got into contacts hurriedly, glancing at the direction of the toilet again and again, while looking for Anvisha's contact, to save it in her phone, just to sift through the reality. She took her phone out to take down Anvisha's number, but while saving it down, she got the sudden realisation that the number was that of Arav himself, saved in the name of Anvisha. This sparked a barrage of questions in her mind. She frowned, as lines appeared on her forehead, she was breathing fast, disquietly she locked the phone and placed it back.

Blankly, she hailed the glow of the moon and the aura, when he came and sat, he asked, "You alright? Seems like you are in deep thoughts?" "Oh yeah, I...I am, no, it's nothing, but your poetry," she smiled at him. They called for the check, left the restaurant, took some ice cream on the way, the one with flakes: his favourite. While on the way to the ice cream man, Anvisha was on her mind the whole time. All this time, she was with him, but not mentally. She acted so normal, not letting him know about her worrying, she duped him with her charm, maybe. He was so happy, so was she, but what was missing there were the answers, answers to be heard, to break down the silence.

It had gotten a bit late for Nasia, and she had some work to be done back home, some sort of art journal. After the ice cream, they got ready to be off, he glanced at her charm for one last time for the night, she let it be, smiling through her eyes, and about to set him free. "Message me once you…", "…once you reach home." She twisted and taunted him to say the same words every time, just to tease him. "Haha, okay, now you know what to do." They hugged, she kissed his cheek, red, and departed.

Just before he stepped into the bus, he took a rose out of the flowers she had given him, and gave it to her. Nasia guffawed and took it. Every time things went perfectly, something bad had to take place, a tragedy in his life. Nasia was so dismayed by the fact of Anvisha, she knew that something was odd about this lady, now it was turning into a belief. For the first time, it was Nasia who was bound in thoughts, finding it hard to come out, thinking about the innocence of Arav and what to do next, for there might be no Anvisha.

When she reached home, she did the work, all disturbed, editing again and again, she knew it was not the time for any work; she was not her anymore, her thoughts were with Anvisha, like Arav. That was where she came to know all the complexity, or maybe some of it, that Arav had been dealing with. Thinking of the entire thing that he dealt with in the name of Anvisha, she lay on the bed, not having changed her clothes still, all messed up, taking a trip down her memory lane about everything that he mentioned about Anvisha. She was lost in flashbacks, looking at the ceiling, as if it was a projector screen. From the very first time he had told her about Anvisha, to the time he talked to her, everything started getting clear to Nasia.

Everything started to make sense to her now, about no picture of hers being in his phone, her absence from social media and now the number. If she was Agoraphobic, how could she work in an atmosphere where she had to deal with other people. In fact, if she was working at all, how could Arav not know about the company, despite being her childhood friend. Even the very thought of them being childhood friends got her right in the nerves. "Wait, a childhood friend she is," she said to herself, as if solving a mystery case. She thought, perhaps understood it, that Anvisha never existed in the first place. She was only playing with him in his brain, where he didn't know what was right anymore.

Not only Anvisha, the art fair, the cemetery, the man who told him the route to the fair and the shop, did they all really exist? Or was it just his imagination, a wild one that could lead to his very own end. Why would a man tell him the way to a cemetery? With a head threatening to burst, she took some pill, not thinking about what to do anymore, changed her clothes and went off to sleep. It was a lot for her to take at that point, forgetting about all the romance of the night, she had gotten carried away with the storm.

Even after taking the pill, her head felt too heavy to sleep, she felt as if she was falling without stopping or hitting any bottom. In the middle of the night, she held her head, it was not good for her health to wake up all of a sudden, even after having taken the pills for sleeping and headache. It was eating her, she embraced herself and told herself that it would be alright soon. Beckoning her own, before getting off again, Nasia dropped a text to her sister, not Aria though, as she didn't want her to be involved in a worried situation like this one.

She woke up the next morning, not with the alarm but because of a rat who had just broken a glass. With blurry eyes, squeezing, she made a weird face at the broken glass, and yelled, "Not again, you bastard." She got up to clean it, before it could hurt her.

It was 8:30 in the morning. The streets, roads, stations were all busy, with everyone rushing to their work, while she vacuumed the pieces together, knowing that Arav would still be asleep at that time. Nasia decided not to go to bed again, as it would be a lazy day then and she didn't want to spend time that way. She took a shower and then had breakfast. Turning on the TV in the background, she started with her journals, the work that had been left pending since the previous night, for she had received e-mails too, asking her to send the journals ASAP. Holding a clip with her lips, she tied her hair and made a call to her colleague to tell them that the work was done.

To feel no stones on her head, she went into her room of art, took a canvas to create an abstract piece. She started with colours, using a blue and red coloured brush to making a curve and a circle in that semi curve, she proceeded to make it, blank minded, it was just him, then another wave under that circle, which looked more like an eye. She heard something, some voice coming from the hall, maybe the TV she had left turned on. She went towards the hall to find out that it was her phone, she rushed towards it, wiping her hands over the clothes she had been wearing for the art, to find out that it was her sister, to whom she had left a message. "Hey, Nasia, oh dear, how are you?" she said, before letting her sister say anything.

"Haha, hi Samaira, I am good, what about you, bitch? It's been long since we last met, I am a bit mad, to tell you the truth," she said, excited to hear her beauteous voice after a week.

"No, baby, you know my work sucks at times, but it's okay, I had to give you a surprise, but I think I should tell you now."

"Oh, a surprise? Are you alright? A surprise, really? What? A box of melted chocolates again?" she asked, remembering the last time she had got a surprise by her.

"Haha, oh dear, you still remember that. You know, it was in a hurry and I didn't want you to be upset, haha. No, it's more than that, I am coming tomorrow, and what a coincidence, you messaged me just a day before."

"WHAT, really? Whoa, how happy am I! What a fate, haha. Damn, I can't wait for you to arrive, actually I can't wait for my chocolates, haha."

"Nasia, I know. But wait, are you alright? The message you sent last night, what is it? Why were you feeling messed up?"

"Oh, Samaira, it's Arav, the guy I befriended some time ago, and he's a great person I've ever come across, it's about him, I'll tell you once you get here. God, I am so happy."

"Aye, seems like my girl's got a man, huh? Haha, okay, we'll figure out whatever it is, dear. I need to leave now, see you tomorrow, baby."

"Yeah, bye, take care." After a moment, she realised how badly she needed help. The reason she was not involving her best mate into it was just to spare her her worry and not to disturb her work because of her. She decided to tell her soon, once the matter got a positive insight overall.

Arav seemed oddly distrait that morning, he had received a mail from the publishing company about his poetry that had gotten published in their journals. They had asked him to meet them as they wanted him to write for a book for them, asking for three poems and two short stories. All he was thinking at that time was about the contract they wanted him to get in, and it was not an easy one, they want it all in a week. However, their contract offered him a great pay.

Pay was the thing that didn't matter to him all that much in the name of writing and art, he only mulled whether he should or should not accept it as it gave him the chance to get recognised for it, and it was one of the opportunities for him to get in. He wrote back to them with his contact details, asking them to brief him about the concept and theme. It was a reading day that day, and the weather was as usual, breezing. He picked up the phone first to see if there was any message unread. What he was hoping for, was her. When he saw that there was none, he dropped her a text regarding the mail he had received by the publisher. He went back to his reading, and it was so soothing that he didn't even feel that he was really there, or reading the book itself.

The very ideology of an old kind of new started occurring to him, he swallowed the very essence of it, slowly letting it enter into his veins. The old was the time when it had been so untwined and now it was all disturbed, outlooking the fact of how it was all messed up now, the language of love and the value of time, pieces of hatred and the stumbling for messages to be delivered, from the whole old scenario to the distraught of old by the new. It all made sense at that time, now it was all frenzied.

The writing of old, that many periods ago was the writing of truth, knew the language of battling with the words, to serve as the best and get a reward by the king, queen, or the public in return. It doesn't make sense now. Not just the writing of today, but the sense of words, they knew well the concept of delivery then, and here we are.

What in wrath one can say, what in jealousy one can redeem, what in the name of hospitality one can know the language of kind while being out of the mental zone of understanding others, their concept and reason of their words. To make head or tail of the dancing leaves on the music of this beautiful wind that is blowing to touch the surface of the very roots of the joy to calm down the thunder of sorrows. How the wind is culpable of or standing behind the reason of the delightfulness of others, flurry of air. There's everything we have is connected to the other, in this or the other way, everything we do, we receive, we hear, we say is somewhere connected deep down to the reason of any happening surrounding us. The concept of everything related to the spiritual realm, not the blind-folded trust in the mighty and its power, but the karma, the order of spirits and all.

It was so messy in his own thoughts, it was his thoughts that were writing him down today, he was in his own words today, splintered ink of thoughts he was becoming, going deep down to the roots of facts, truth, lies, complexity of understanding behaviour and mind. As he turned the pages, it went more vicariously wide, like words intercepted, but to let him fall in the deep, deep cave from where he couldn't climb the way up, for his every attempt to climb led him deeper, cut off form the sane, to feel the insanity of the insane. Words he read out loud within, formed into wilderness.

It was when he beheld himself masked, a grey-black cloth covering his face, leaving his eyes, having a spade in his hands and a voice screaming to him to dig faster, when he looked to the ground, it changed into an ocean, like comically changing settings, but he was living it, he looked around and there was nothing but sea and a sun hiding under black clouds, he tried to reach out to water, to feel if it was real, instant; when he touched it, the setting changed again, and he was in the Himalayas, for as far as he could lay his sight, it was all mountains, he didn't touch anything now, even the rose and the lily, he stopped there, looked around, stood still to see, to know what it was, to feel the aura of alienation. The sky started falling upon him, he could feel it, as if the ceiling was falling, closer and more, then it fell upon him, so hard, that he was in sane now, it was his ceiling, he was back at home. A notification, that is, a message tone had called him back from the world he had just gotten himself into.

"What are you saying? Really? It is the window to the world, you know that, wow, congrats dear, call me once you done reading." She meant the happiness. It was her message that had brought him back.

Arav placed a bookmark in the book, put it back at the shelve, washed his face to freshen up and made a call to her, telling her that he had already shared his contact, and was waiting for their reply on the concept. He could feel the shiver in her voice, wondering if it was the excitement or if something was bothering her. Poor him, he took it as excitement, unknown to the fact it was he himself, who had shaken her beautiful focus to the wonderment of his own condition.

Nasia asked to catch up with him the next day, but didn't tell him about her sister being there too, she wanted him to meet her as a surprise, he didn't even know if she had a sister, and to retain the amazement, she didn't mention it either. They talked for a while, he told her about the book he had been reading, but they both knew that it was way more than that, but no one said it for the time being. As she listened to his rustic, wavy, yet calm voice, it was unalike in her reverie, she was conjecturing as if Anvisha had called him, as he thought it to be, she was about to ask him this, but it would have been so irrelevant to ask him simultaneously, so she just heard him talk and talk.

A tight loving hug is the way to calm an ongoing storm sometimes, but it was her voice that was enough to make him stay in the place where she was, her hug would have been his heaven and an official love of her would not be his drug, for it would be his stable breath. After they cut the call, he looked outside the window, there she was, a bird who loved to live there with her chicks, what he called by was, son and daughter, he then saw the children playing in the park down there, what he didn't know was that he was thinking he might spot the old man again, not to talk to him, but just to see him help someone else like him.He had decided to tell Nasia the next day, about the old man, he had never told her, as he thought it to be his sane of blues, but he knew he existed, the man with mighty powers, as if he was the person who lived in the statue of angels, for angels lived in disguise, this man lived in it, in the disguise of an old man.

Chapter Six

Art speaks many languages through art itself, this fascination kept her up all night, and the obvious reason of Arav condition. Even before shower, she went into her art room first, took the canvas, and continued the piece she had started early in the day, she observed what she had done earlier, and she had no idea about it, but it was so in her, if she started, her will did not allow her to start anew before completing the one left.

Using blue and red colour, she splintered the glittering in the wave that had been under the circle beforehand. It was her mind, her way of making a piece. Then a big line she drew, mixing red and white, and making stems from that line, didn't look like a tree though, but those were leaves on the stems in sky blue watercolour. Lost in her own, she forgot about the time and indulged in making the piece, she was just about to end, just a final touch that she had to give by adding some drops of watercolour onto some parts of it, when she heard a smooth bash on the door, a 'trpp trpp', letting her know that someone's there – she heard knocks. The very first thought that came to her was, 'It must be her, Samaira.'

She laid the brush down and rushed towards the door, not considering to do anything before; to get the door, unlocked it and there she was, standing still, wearing a huge, huge smile, untied hair, white tee, in a denim jacket and washed denim jeans, white shoes, holding a box that was gift wrapped in yellow and pink. "Oh girl, look at you, haha, hi baby," Samaira remarked, as there was paint colour all over her face in marks. With a glow in her eyes, she hugged her, not caring about the paint on her.

"Samaira," she partly screamed her name, before she could say anything, she hugged her, and welcomed her home. "What were you doing, dear? Were you up-to your art? Oh, surely you were," she said, still holding her hand.

"Haha, yeah, you know it, I totally forgot about you, haha," Nasia said, feeling foolish.

"You really did? Oh, I need to hand over this gift to someone else then."

"Hey, haha. How was your flight. anyway? And you must be hungry, you left early in the morning, wait, let me get you something first."

"Nasia, look at you, go and get a bath first, ass. I'll get something by myself, am I coming here for the first time, lol?"

"Oh, yeah, haha, sorry, I'll just come, go and make yourself comfortable, I'll be there." She left everything, the art too, thinking to complete it later, and went off to bath. Nasia was so happy to see her, the old charm she desired always, and the comfort she received by her hug. She left a message to Arav to come to her place instead, and they would go from her place, adding her address and adding that she was going for a shower.

While Nasia was in the shower, Samaira changed and made herself a sandwich, and prepared the stuff for pasta for both of them, as Nasia too hadn't had anything. With a sandwich in her hand, she went to her art room, to hail the real beauty of the time being, of-course, she had all her right by her, being an elder sister and for the love bond they shared. Tying up her long hair, amazed by the pieces she saw, she then laid her eyes on the piece she had been on early that morning before getting the door, it was so obvious as the paint was still wet. In the deep cave of ruminating and apprehending the piece she just has created, it seemed complete, but she felt something missing, without thinking even for once, she picked up the same brush, and used a watercolour, sparkles and beige, and outlined the part of stems, and the cloud, moon, and of the semi curve, that looked perfect. She filled the places that looked undone. It was so beautiful to see, under one curve, that was of sanity, how our pupils become, and when it rains, how the night moon changes it colour and shines through, and the line was actually a wall, from where the stems were occurring, asking to rescue them, as the fine wall covered the tree, which was cut in half now.

The piece was simple, it was just the chaos of her mind which was clear in there. Samaira went to the bedroom and relaxed there. When Nasia came out of the shower, she freaked out, she had not expected her in the room. “What?”

“You freaked me out, God, haha. Oh, wait, did you have something?”

“Ahh, yeah Nasia, I did, and have prepared for a pasta too, you just need to cook it, to be served fresh with fresh taste.”

“Oh, wow, nice, thank you, my chef, haha, how did you know I didn’t have any breakfast?”

“Just a guess. You were in your art room in the morning, dear, and I saw your pieces, and the one you were on, I completed it, it was done, but with some unfilled things, so I thought of…”

"Wait, what? Ahh, you are amazing, now I know how much I missed you," she said, placing her towel in the bucket of laundry. "How is it, I don't really know what I was doing there."

"It was perfect, dear, in-fact, amazing, that made me run my hand over it. And hey, your phone was vibrating; I was too lazy to get that, sorry."

"Really? Thank you, I want to see what you added up by your beautiful thought process." She felt good, she liked it when her sister played her hand over her pieces, it was her only, who had motivated Nasia to believe in her drams, art. "Oh, the phone, it must be him, lazy you, bitch, haha."

"Oh yeah, you were telling me something about this person, what is it?" she asked, curiously.

"Oh, my dear, haha yes, I forgot to tell you, let's have this conversation over pasta, come." It was him on the phone, he told her that he was on his way and asked why she had called him home that day, though he was excited to see her home, and her too. What an ease she was at after seeing Samaira, her nerves, which had been on such discomfort, worried, were now calm and peaceful.

Nasia went to her art room first, to see what Samaira had added, and she got surprised by the little elements of truth she had added, she had a similar idea in her mind, but not as beautiful as this, she told Samaira about the same thinking process, which was not as amazing as hers, and how glad she was to see it. Samaira served the pasta to her and to herself, and there she started telling her about where they had met Arav, and what was wrong with him and her friend, Anvisha, who didn't exist, as she had cross-checked everywhere before jumping to this conclusion. She was dismayed to hear this disturbing situation of Arav, Nasia told her everything, from the type of love and the writer he was, to his mental state. When Samaira asked if she loved him, or was infatuated with him, she nodded to her, and it was a yes, she was infatuated with him, saying that this love would be a bit complex, but the love was growing beneath them, she knew. She understood every word Nasia said.

"He will be alright soon, you are with him, baby, it's okay."

"He will be here anytime soon, I asked him to come home; I wanted you both to meet as a surprise, haha."

They shared everything, about her work and how she was doing lately, it was going so smooth, they were both glad as Samaira was going to stay for a week, after which, she would get back to her work, but in London itself. Her phone started ringing, she picked up, he said "I think I am at the right place, and this door seems like there's a beauty who lives here, and it is protecting you."

"Haha, Arav, haha, it was amazing, wait."

"Was that Arav?"

"Oh, yeah, let me take him in. Actually no, you take him in, it would be fun, haha"

"Yeah haha, it would be, wait."

Samaira opened the door with a serious face, and there he was standing, blushing for no reason, with a roll in his hand which he stopped eating upon seeing an unknown person. For a moment he thought he was at the wrong place, but nothing came out of his mouth as he got struck by the beauty that resembled that of someone very loveable to him. "Yes," she asked, frowning.

"Uh, I think I...I am at wrong place, sorry," he said, but before turning back, he asked, "Do you know Nasia? She gave me this address, either I am or her address is mistook here." He looked at her nervously and wondered who she was, and whom she resembled of. She, Samaira, making her voice a bit heavy, said, "You are at the right place. I can be your Nasia if you want me to be," still holding the door, and making some weird pose she added, " Nasia is just an updated version of me."

He didn't get a thing she said, but screamed 'what' inside, his face went all pale when she said she could be her Nasia, for a moment he felt utterly frustrated but couldn't be so towards her. "What?" he said in wonder, 'an updated version, what's that?' He guffawed but was still confused about what to say or whether to just leave. She could tell from his face that he thought her quite weird. "Won't you eat your roll now?" she asked again in a heavy voice, "Come inside, let's eat together." At this point, he was so gone, didn't know what to say anymore. "You're so weird, shit, what are you saying?" he asked thunderously, yet smoothly, still trying to get who she resembled with.

The time he turned back, saying sorry to Samaira, unknown to the fact that she was her sister, Nasia knew him so well, that she knew he was about to leave now, so she suddenly shouted, "Aye, haha, wait Arav." A familiar voice, oh, he breathed in her voice. "Nasia?" he stopped and looked back at the door, Samaira was laughing so heartedly, and Nasia was standing there too, calling him in, laughing. "You are so innocent, Arav," Samaira said.

"Look what you did there, haha, you almost made him drown in the wonder of existentialism, Samaira, but it was so amazing, haha, damn. You are so weird, lol."

"Haha, yeah, look at him, shit, sorry, come in."

He had no idea what on earth was going on, who was she, he smiled embarrassingly, and looked at his roll that he didn't want to eat anymore, thinking what he should do now, he went in, looking at Samaira confusedly and then at Nasia, they were laughing so bad. "Oh, wait," he screamed so loud that they stopped and looked at him. "What?" Nasia asked, while Samaira continued to laugh.

"What, haha, wait, is she your sister? Damn, the whole time I was wondering whom she mirrored. Now I can see both of you, it's of you, haha, damn, you guys look so similar."

After a moment of silence, he started laughing out loud, yet nervously, as he was meeting her for the very first time. "Now I know, haha, by the thing you said, that she is your updated version, haha." They burst out in laughter on hearing this.

"Wait, I didn't hear that, Samaira, you literally said that?" Nasia asked, while holding her stomach aching from laughter.

An updated version of her actually made more sense. When they settled down from their elation, she introduced him to Samaira, her elder sister. Nasia took the roll from him to put it away as he really didn't want to have anymore of it. She now told him why she had really called him to her place, to let him meet her Sister, and as he had never visited her place before, that too. When he asked Nasia why she had never told him about her sister, he received an expected reply, that he had never asked, neither did she remember. Nasia took him to the couch, made him comfortable, she knew that he must have wanted coffee. "Well, a coffee by your hands sounds so amazing, I would drink it all day long, I know, thank you, yeah." She then asked Samaira if she wanted one, as they had just had their food. "Oh yeah, if he is in desire of coffee by your hands, I think I need it too, haha."

She went to the kitchen to make them coffee and left them both to talk, as they were. Samaira told him about her arrival early that day, as she had been busy travelling because of work. "Work? What work is it?" he asked.

"I am in event management, there's a team I handle."

"Oh, that means you are the senior most there."

"Oh yeah, that's right, so I got time to visit her after a bit long, and gladly, I'll be here in London now, till at least the next big event comes up, as most big events have wrapped up."

"Great, it is amazing."

She asked about his writings, as Nasia had already told her about him, everything, she was observing her, she knew the complexity of human behaviour so beautifully as she had studied Psychology a lot, and that her work was related to soothing the mind, while being at any kind of event, excited or boring. They shared their intellectual thoughts on almost everything, like he did with Nasia. Samaira was so similar to her, even her sane, it was so obvious to say that yes, she was her updated version, just in age; they shared almost the same thoughts on everything. She, Nasia, got them a coffee. "Here you go with the hard reality (strong coffee) Arav, putting it on the table and here is yours, dear."

They got so indulged in their talks, and more when they sat together that they forgot to show him their home, as he had come there for the very first time. "Oh, sorry, don't you want to look around my house? I forgot, haha." "Oh yeah, obviously, they say that there lays another world in the house of an artist." What an excitement was running under him to explore an artist's home. She took him around to show her home, in the very end they entered the art room.

When he entered the art room, boom, he went blank, not being able to come down from his thoughts of being there, in her room. If an artist shows you their room, never doubt their love, as their room is their inner self, like a body on bed in a love act, like the honey that bees collect. That one room, that one place is bigger than all; you can't look at the real person more lively than by being present and standing in them, in their world, from all the outer to all the personal. Samaira was along with him, observing him, his mouth was literally open, and he laughed nervously when she remarked on it.

Nasia was so happy to have him in her heart, where she breathed. He shared his thoughts regarding some of the art peices.

When Samaira reflected that he observed in most kind way, she, Nasia told her about his viewing of art by telling her about the art fair, where they had encountered each other for the second time, and he had been the only one who got her art so amazingly and aptly. "Oh, I can see a writer there now." He saw more and more of it, as she described her art to him, when and at what moment she had made a particular piece, briefing him a bit on it.

The aura there was so astonishing that he didn't even realise what he hailed in there, he told them about what he had gone through while reading some book earlier that day when he received her message, and where he had been in his sanely imagination, and now he was there again, as he was seeing piece by piece, tripping again onto the journey's he had been at, early, a morning ago.

She, Nasia, had to buy the colours and stuff for her art, and some other the things related to her work. It was noon now, about to turn into an evening breath, when she asked Samaira if she was coming with them. "Oh, no, sorry baby, but I have to meet my colleague in like half-an hour, I'll catch up with you guys late in the evening, is that okay?" "Ah, I can understand your dynamic work, okay ass, but not so late, bind up your work, whatever it is, I need no hustle, tomorrow must be our free day."

"Aww, haha, yeah sure, baby, you must leave now, I'll get ready with some work to leave, yeah." Just before they left, she said, "It was really amazing to know you Arav, really, I must say you both interlink in each of your psyche, haha, I'll catch up." He remarked the same and they left to get her stuff, or on another date, maybe.

Taking a bus to a nearby mall near canary wharf, she talked about her sister, and how he liked her and how she really could make one think about her, Nasia. It was romantic as earlier, every-time they met it turned into something romantic, she tried to dive into him and his condition, wondering if he had talked to Anvisha, and she asked about her again. "I don't know why you are asking about her again? She has been behaving a bit changed since the time I told her about you, let her come back in her zone, even I want her to meet you." She could clearly see the avoidance of Anvisha to meet her, oh, actually his subconscious imagination named Anvisha, as she knew it now.

They entering the mall talking about a myriad of things, when she asked about the previous day's mail, had they replied to him. "No, they will within three days, it said on the mail." She took him to the shop in the mall where she shopped for her art things, all the colours and whatever stuff of use in art, alien to Arav, he didn't know what she was asking for, he was feeling so lame to be there with unheard names of the things, she laughed real hard on this when he told her after she had shopped. "You'll get used to it now, dear," she said staring right into his eyes, so full of love and excitement, maybe a birth of a new love story, every time they met.

"Hey, what if we go to your place now, while Samaira gets done with her ass work? I want to see your writer's place, I think." "Wow, why not? I was really about to ask you for this, yeah let us go to my place after you work." "Yeah, sure, there's just one more thing I need to get for Aria."

"Oh yeah, Aria, where is she? Let's meet her, no?" "Haha, yes, we will be meeting her tomorrow, Samaira too wants to meet her, she really likes her, now she likes you too." He blushed, now for a reason.

After being done with her work, they left for his place. On their way, he realised that he didn't tell her about the old man yet. "Nasia." "Yeah?"

"I wanted to tell you about this man, an old man, I encountered several times, two-three actually, and he is the man with every bit of knowledge on earth, he can read you, can solve any of your problems, we'll meet him soon, if we get a chance to see him." She listened about this old man so closely, and thought it might be his imagination too, He said, "Sometimes, I think he lives in my thoughts and appears when I feel stuck, but then I think no, he is real, I've seen him helping others, form my window." She tried to believe him, as she didn't want to hurt his sentiments, and perhaps he was real, as what was not real, Anvisha, was existent for him, and what was there, he thought it to be his imagination. "I would like to meet him, wow, sounds so beautiful." "Yeah, we soon will."

Neither had realised while heading to his home that they had held each other's hands, unknowingly, they felt diffident, but loved it inside, they again did it, this time being sentient. As the touch they felt, they tasted it, not only a person but both, as if their skin was asking them to be in contact, as if it had been urging for it for so long. Surveying other's eyes, seeing the pupil growing bigger, she ardours her own lips while looking at him, so passionately. And he was totally lost in her charm of alluring in the shade of dark of the evening. They reached his home, he had pointed form the street, "See, that's my window." "Oh, I've seen your home now, let's go somewhere else, haha." Arav got this joke a bit late and laughed on his own. He took the lift after days.

He Unlocked the door, she was excited to explore his place now, to meet the writer's inner space. "After you, ma'am," he said, gesturing with both hands. She walked in, oh, the smile she got was so infectious, looked back for him, he closed the door, holding a bag of the stuff she had shopped, from her, and placed it on the chair. It was so unlike this evening; she was there for the very first time, seeing his home, the kitchen was so clean and everything was in its place, unlike the time when Anvisha was there, earlier. Stepping ahead into the room, he went to his bedroom to get something from his closet, leaving her exploring, there was not much to see, as there were not many rooms, just two, and a kitchen, and a small hall. She saw the room where the couch was, where he spent most of his day, from a distance, he said, it was the place where he spent most of his time. "Oh, I can see it, your book is still here and the stuff is a bit crumbled, fatty ass." He stood there, still having a paper in his hand to give to her, but waited to let her see his home.

It was not just her seeing his home then, but trying to get to his roots, when she laid her sight on the wall, she saw posters everywhere, full of writings of his and some famous dead poets; amazed she was, it did not look like the zone of one sane living bring in a corrupt human race, full of lies and imagination far, far away from reality and hope. From Robert Burns to Wordsworth, each and every beautiful writing, and then came his. Nasia got a bit alert when she read it -

Oh the rain of despair,
cut my sane to live deeper,
deeper than faith.

Today when I ask you to lie
don't, for I want to see fade for a while,
not exile, but to walk unnumbered miles
to; leave imagination.

It was written with the background of a man looking at a waterfall, and standing at the edge of it, maybe hoping for a fall, or for someone to hold him back, in the shade of sunset.

She decided not to react much, but to see what else; looking at the posters again, the ones left unread; it had mesmerized her but also built a strong worry regarding him, the time she lay her sight over the shelf, she couldn't stop herself from walking to it, from down to up, it was mixed with the design, the design of reading; some were showing the spine, where some were kept there by the pages so that one could not read the name, he has done it for himself, to pick onto the books blindly, to read, whatever came in his hand, not judging or for random readings. 'Isn't it so amazing to keep it this way,' she said to herself. It was so beautifully placed, she was flabbergasted for a moment, there was a glow of sparkles in her eyes.

Something was there, something that can't be described or written, maybe. He put the paper in the pocket and walked to her, calmly, slowly to reach, she was touching the books, feeling the essence, having a glow in her eyes, open mouth, that of amazement, he walked towards her, blankly; he didn't even think about it for once, reaching out to her, held her from her hand, that was on the shelve in the touching act. She glanced at him with a smile, asking what, guffawed, but got still when she looked into his eyes, to fall in him, to find her in him, to reach out for her, that lied somewhere in the hail, right this moment.

As if time had stopped, the sudden sibilant of breeze ceased somewhere in the moment, or the sin that was about to be committed, later acceptable. Not saying a word, the breaths grew heavy, as he gazed at her more and more, she looked at his lips, and her eyes screamed to take a step further. He knew the complexity of this, and the harsh consequences, and he was not ready to take the burden, keeping in mind his mental state, but it could even be his gateway to the new world – all the rush in her mind, but she let it be.

He called her closer by taking her hand to let her take a hold of him, grabbed her by her waist with both hands, feeling her curves for the first time, her eyes were so in the moment, clasping his shirt, on the chest, not making eye contact for she couldn't control to create another fine art, but he was ready to write a story, the story of souls that touched the marrow of love, like the ink seeping into blood, and blood written on the pages of history.

The scintillation of her eyes, and the shimmer in his, not widely, but as if the perfume of a forest in the perfect shade of night, they were breathing, her shining pink lips to her face charm, and the emotions his face shed, no words but just the blood rush, and time itself lay in the fine gap between their lips.

Nasia wanted to fall now, forgetting all about Anvisha, she just wanted to route down the map of his heart, by this act, she definitely could reach the roots of his reversal psychological problem; above all, she desired to let it happen, to let the sweet taste of him run over her tongue.

He pulled her closer to conclude the space left amidst their souls to meet, sensuously she closed her eyes, as if frame by frame, ready to fall in him; his breaths were wanting her more, her breath to take in, to breathe him more, ardently he shut his eyes, as if the two stars collide, but salubriously. Unfurling their mouths, to let her take the lower and taste her upper soft lip, dainty drop they sucked. Disparate heavy breathes, she placed her hand on his neck, then wraps around his hair, clenching fingers, and with the other hand, still held onto his shirt at the chest, but now she placed her hand on his heart, to feel each and every beat of it, to let her own beats dance on his.

Nothing was in their mind, but it was the moment, just the moment dripping on them, when he felt her face form her jaw line, to her ear he reached to kiss, she did the same, relishing his neck, biting and biting, while he was still at her ear, "Uhh," his breathed by her jaw, for she had bit a piece of him, her fingers ran over his face to discern him and then on his, wrapping. They stopped for a moment, looking into each other's eyes, intemperate inhalation; Oh, the perfect baby pink of their lips, all wet, and his neck hurting a little, by the taste that she had took.

Latched deep emotions in their exhalation, the rush was so alluringly intense that they couldn't think of anything but to get into one another, it started again, she took the upper, he took the lower, tongues rolling in the mouth, as if the tongue was imbibing the spirit, more intensely this time, her grip got strong and scratched his back, whereas his hands were as soft as a hand on a new-born, they ran over her curves as if he knew the terrain already, the roads, the back-road, turn by turn. He mapped her, she traced him, couldn't come to an end but it had to now, else it would've lasted for hours, they wanted to stop but they also wanted to let the sin be committed. They wanted to cease the moment right then, but letting the moment commit them, apparently –they wanted it so bad.

She exhaled, "I think we...we should," she paused and kissed him again, tasting every essence of his spirit on her lips, "We should stop now, I think," –still with unequal breaths. He nodded, "Yeah, it must."

What had just taken place was not just a moment they had had, that lasted for some minutes, but was the time and the fate that were imprinting them to read the souls of two celestial bodies. The silence was unquiet; the pervasive substance that had to be there after a moment of intimacy was not there; maybe, maybe because the zone of opulence they shared was so unique. They stood still as if the wind had stopped, as if all the rings of Saturn had turned to stone, motionless. Discharging from the link they were in, they started blushing, while he removed with his finger a twirl of hair that was on her lips.

Talking through their eyes after the act, as if the exile of humankind was to be told, not coming to anything, no words to be shared, "Do you...do you want fruits?" asked Arav. "What? Haha, Arav." It was so bad, she turned, even she didn't know what to say, but it was really bad. "Fruits, really? Haha, it's okay, we don't need to, baby." That change from 'dear' to 'baby' was so subtle, maybe it had to happen as they both knew what they had for each other in them, they had no need to confess, it had been done.

They didn't talk about it much as they really lived it, "Words, oh words, I have unnumbered scales as I hold them to praise you more and more, Nasia, need I say more?" he just said in his own way, as he couldn't claim it directly, being shy. "Wow, beautiful, Arav, you have said a million things in this itself, I love you too, haha. Man, my man, you are a muse too." It was all so ease that they had in each other, their muses. Now it had been confessed through words as well.

He sat on the couch, with a blank mind, she went to the kitchen, poured water for herself and in another glass for him, they talked about the universe and stillness and the voices they heard of their breaths, and now it had started, the endless talking from the goddesses to the muses, from spirituality to the art there was in myths. In the mean time, her phone rang, it was Samaira, Nasia said to him, "Oh great, she must be free now, we should leave." "Yeah."

"Hello, baby, I am free now, where are you guys?" she asked excitedly.

"Oh, we are at Arav's home, let's meet near the central station in 30?"

"Haha, yeah in 30, done," Samaira, being more experienced, knew what must have been going on there.

They left his home, Nasia took her bag, not thinking for a moment about the thing that had just taken place, but about his condition, to reach out for his roots, but she knew that she could treat him, and make him recover, even if it took all her heart-beats. Sharing their thoughts on the acts of intimacy of the old era, they reached the central and saw her, Samaira was sitting at the bus stop before them, talking to some lady, pointing at some direction. "Haha, as if she knows all the routes, sometimes she even forgets the way to my home," mocked Nasia.

"How was it, what did you guys do, except the bag that I am seeing right there," she seemed so happy, that Nasia couldn't stop herself from saying, "Leave the bag, you seem high on some ecstasy, what is it?"

"Haha, you know me so well." He just looked at them, alien to their talks. "Nothing, it was just an event for the cause of cancer and a food festival in Paris, and it's a huge deal we got."

"Amazing, great, yeah, I am happy for you," Nasia's happiness grew a little dim at the thought of her sister leaving soon. "Why, Nasia, haha, it's okay, I didn't tell you the best part of it yet, the thing I'll tell over dinner, you'll go crazy." Samaira knew well how to keep the suspense on and make the other person crave for it in wait.

"That's not fair, what is it? Damn you, bitch, why do you always tell everything in pieces? Tell me, haha." "Aye, haha, let it be, let's get this out over food, I am hungry again."

"When are you not?" The sisters then laughed together in unison.

She told them about the boring yet joyful meeting, and asked her about her art events, suggesting her to dive into the world of it, and accept the art collectors' offers, as it was the best way to be known in the big industry and she had already earned a name for herself at a big level. Arav suggested the same to her, but when he said it, she came to him, for his writings and works and to get them published in literary journals and to accept the offers of other publishers too, the bond between Art and Writing has always been praised.

It was an indirect indication that she knew about their love for each other and accepted it too, no one was that dumb between them, to not have gotten this indirect yet clear approach. He nodded, so did Nasia, and they burst into laughter. "Where the fuck are we heading, Nasia?" Samaira asked, as she had no clue. "See, I told you, she doesn't even know her own way and was helping others navigate, haha."

"What, oh, you saw that, haha, I knew the place she was asking the directions for, so shut it, haha." "Oh you guys, haha, what's the plan, dear?"

"I am thinking of getting something like Pizza or maybe some street food, and let's have it at Trafalgar Square, hmm?"

"Whoa, that sounds nice, yeah, cool, we should do that," he remarked. "Yeah, I like it too."

"You have to, Samaira, you have to, I am still waiting for what you haven't told us yet."

"Haha, over food, baby."

Observing the shade of night imprinting on the streets so massively, and the busy lives surround them, many thoughts having many faces within one, everything made sense to her, Samaira, when he told her about the story of a guy drowning, no one was there to help him, when he saw a feather floating, the very first thought that hit him was, 'If this lifeless abandoned thing can float, why can't an alive creature like me in a corrupted human race can?' He stopped his breath to act like he was dead, so he could float, not knowing how to swim, but he was such a fool to do such stupidity with heavy thoughts, as he was already dead in there, when he looked back to see how far he had arrived, he laid his sight over his own body. Nasia didn't really listen to the whole thing, instead, she was discerning his thoughts at the level of abstraction, while Samaira did both. In the mean-time, they got pizza and some drinks, along with french fries, and went to sit at the Trafalgar Square.

There were many people sitting there already, as usual, but not too many, as there was none at the corner facing Big Ben, Samaira got on the statue of the lion first, and then pulled Arav and Nasia up too. Sitting there, it was quite windy and cold, they unpacked all the food stuff they had got, and satisfied their hunger. The sisters glanced at him and said, "If you still feel hungry after this monster pizza, I am telling you, you need to start eating plants more, they are everywhere, you can get the leafs for the time at least." Cracking jokes, they shared words about the beautiful world with no humans on it. "What is it? The thing you were going to tell, speak now." "Haha, yeah, okay dear."

"The Paris thing I told you about, I won't be going there alone. Having most of the rights in my hand, I have booked a place for you two, as a token of gift, tickets and everything has been done, and I don't want to hear a no," she said, without letting them say a word, as she saw Arav about to build a trail of questions from within.

"It's me who has organised this, say, a sponsored trip for

you both along with me, and it's just about three days, yeah, am I clear?" she asked, clearing her throat afterwards.

Nasia was on cloud nine to hear it, she was so happy to know that her sister had actually done that for them, she obviously didn't ask anything, instead, told her that she could go to some art event that was being held there on the same dates, she was excited to attend and meet many famous artists there, and what delighted her the most was knowing that her sister has accepted him, by showing this gesture.

"But wait, I can't, see, I do not like it, why did you book it for me? Like, why am I that important for you, you hardly know me, still?" he asked in wonder.

"When did I say that you are of any importance to me, but as being hers; when you actually are a part of mine too. It's because I liked you and her choice, you. It might not be an official relationship as of now, I know, but I know it would be, or perhaps it is." He didn't say anything, but just looked at Nasia, who smiled at him, with an approach in her eyes to just accept it. And he did the same.

She had really amazed them both by telling them about this trip and the great big elation of Nasia was not coming down, Paris was the city for them to be, as they had the real sense of love and art and fashion, oh, the city of everything. They came back to being normal again, and started making plans for the trip, talking about beautiful words by sharing real beautiful thoughts.

Nasia gave her clip to him to keep safe, knowing that he wouldn't give it back, as he liked to keep things from her, like her very heart. He felt the paper in his pocket again, remembering that he had forgot to give it toher, took out the paper, and give it to her, saying that it was the same poetry that he had recited, with some extended stanzas and wanted to hand it over to the very inspiration behind the piece. She took the paper, Samaira drew closer next to her, waiting for her to unfold it when Nasia stopped to look at a distracted Arav, looking at someone who was standing right at the other corner, staring at them.

Thick kohl in her eyes, a purple shade of lipstick, in a white and blue dress, an unfamiliar face to recognise, he tried to focus on her to know who she was and why she was looking at them strangely, where the sisters were alien to her, guessing or having an inner sense that there must be a weird kind of relation between Arav and the lady who was staring at them. Her expressionless face came to life, while her smile grew bigger and bigger, and then a tear dropped.

In cloudless climes, how can it even be possible to have stars beneath, in the shade of sombre? Oh, the light might have been distorting the fact of his heed regarding this lady, 'How could it be?' was the question corrupting his mind to react. Reality with fiction, fiction with reality intervened with fantasy, the same fantasy, the imagination he lived, how could it be possible to see that lifeless life so alive, staring right into his eyes, the same face. 'What, you?' he hushed.

Everything got painted when her innocent tear dropped of black, words were echoing in his ears in his own voice, with the laughter of a familiarly unfamiliar voice.

May the charm of lust to be asked

for the strong and a poisonous scar

senses of touch and the bites

in this aura of midnight

will you, will you.

Will I, oh I will, I will to fall that uncloaked till. With laughter and the words of the lady's voice echoes were so loud and deafening. He didn't know anything; it was just the blurred background, focused at the portrait of this lady, looking at him to say something, but couldn't let out as in the moment between, there was so much to take at that time.

The piece of paper with Nasia and Samaira, that remained folded and hung fire to be unfolded with time, seemed as yellow as a dead piece, almost, an abandoned letter.

Chapter Seven

Everything seemed motionless, nothing but eye in eye, all the voices disappeared in that instant, just through the sigh of theirs they talked, tripped down the moment of detailed night, elucidated sin and the guilt of the mighty, from the history to the past. That sight of eyes, in a blink, reckoned beauteous moments; it was nothing other than just an act of need, or desire. There was nothing between them, but he, drowning without being damped, and she, the sorrow she was breathing, two souls, different bodies were sharing the vibes of a scream, and the time it got hooked, their whines, as if a wire connected them from both the sides. From the moment, they met as the wind flowing like a river.

That moment of stillness, in that tiny moment of stillness, they went back to the time it took place in history, for Arav it was still unbelievable to see her, he never thought he had something with a lady who really existed, all this time he thought it was another old nightmare he used to have, before Nasia. How could he not have thought of this, of-course, when he found his bed all alone, just him that morning, that morning when his head was so heavy from having committed something inapt, maybe, but that soon faded away, as he took it to be another vision of his of being sanely false.

In the breeze of winters, how a life should calendar its autumn, the essence of body, and the creature that craved the salty taste of it. In the mist of rain, how not to unbound the bounded line to fly, each and every line he claimed that night still echoes in her somewhere, from his every word to his every touch on her body to scale on the bed of guilt, she knew from the very first moment when they started shedding their clothes, that it might be a trap of guilt, a sober party in a drunk aura. 'Why not the skin tightens itself, why does it need a touch by someone to unfold, to be as soft as the petals of a glorified overrated rose,' she asked, recalling the moment.

'For the life of the unwanted, to the life of strode plain sorrow of death, may the touch be all it wants,' he replied. She was not drunk back then, nor he; it was just the essence of the aura, for she was there to forget some pain she had got from her life, that had entered again that morning, and he was there because Anvisha was not there when he had wanted her, he called her several time to appear in the crowd, but she didn't, she lied to him every single moment, that she would be there whenever he was in need of her, that day she wasn't, again.

They didn't disturb their silence, both the sisters knew how many words were being shared in that moment. "Hello Arav, remember me?" She finally chose to break the silence.

"Hey, oh, it's so blurry, but how could I forget you, Grace," He had an outburst of feeling, that he didn't let out.

"Oh, I am glad you do, how have you been? I am seeing you after ages for the second time, I have tried to find you several times at the same place, but couldn't," she spoke it, the thing that was under her.

"Ah, no yeah, I mean no, I don't go to these places, that was the time of my rant, so I needed to be there I thought, then I met you like I always feel the wind on my face, but you are real, haha," he didn't know if he really said it, but he did anyway.

"I can see that, and those beautiful people there too, I am happy that you are there, where you deserve to be," she said, glancing at Samaira and Nasia, "They are gorgeous." She didn't claim it on their face herself, as she felt it would be bit embarrassing, so she said it to him.

"Oh, haha." He looked at them, total foreigners, not knowing about anything but still they smiled to him. "Yeah, she...they are."

"I can see your 'she and they' there, haha, anyway I am happy for you," she said, hiding something in her, a scream of sorrowful joy. When he asked her about her doings, if she was alright and if everything was great. "I am still on bed-time Arav, destructed totally by the violence of this hateful world towards me, always." She didn't show it, but her tears were dropping unknowingly, in pain.

"I...I...I think that I should go once and for all, like earlier, and sorry for that time, I was on the shame of a guilt trap, and think I am again, I should not disturb you guys, have a great time ahead, bye guys." She drew closer to him, and hugged him, he was so destroyed within and shocked, but he showed that was alright at that time, hugging her back, and she kissed his cheeks and glanced at Nasia, before she left.

He couldn't stop her, for he shouldn't, as he saw her leaving. Arav felt such pity for her, that it almost made him cry, coming out from the realisation that yes, she existed, the time he was with Grace in bed, she really had existed, but swayed his emotions as if it was she, Grace, who had chosen life to be like this, he couldn't help her now, cause she didn't want to come back from her state of pain and joy to forget everything and again be on the bed of pain.

He bear-hugs Nasia first, and then Samaira. "Oh, sorry for that guys, it was more real than I thought, anyway let's go." "yeah, it's totally fine Arav," said Samaira.

"Yeah, it's fine baby." They knew about his mental state, how delicate he was and his state was, they didn't ask anything, instead, they left the place, picking up some chocolates from the grocery store nearby. "Oh, have you seen the poetry yet?" "Oh no, no we didn't, cause of that. Wait, let's see now, till the bus comes." She opened the page, there were two folded page. "What's the second one for?" she asked, but he didn't really react much, as he himself was not sure what it was. "Second page?"

There were two titles, on each page, one read 'O'love, my love' and the second one was unfamiliar, with 'A night of Grace' written on it. Samaira and Nasia looked at each other, "Arav, what is this for?"

Innocent, he didn't know about it, hidden under the one, as they were both at the same place. "Shit, sorry for that, damn, that was the poetry I had written for the lady we just met up there, Grace, and all through my past time I thought it was my imagination that I had met a lady like her ever, and we had some moments together, but today, I too was shocked to see her, standing before me, real as hell. Sorry Nasia, I didn't tell you about this, as I didn't know it by myself."

She really didn't feel upset at all, knowing that he had had some moment with the lady unknown, she was not the type of lady who took some things so viciously, she acted so cool, along with Samaira, they had some other state of mindset regarding all this stuff. All she wanted to do was to get in him, to take out from him Anvisha, who was still alive in him.

When they read the poetry he had written for Nasia, she felt beautiful as the last time, when she heard the piece for the first time, he recited the same to her again, but there were some add-ons that she liked. “What, you serious? It’s so beautiful, Arav, I wish someone would write this kind of stuff for me too,” Samaira said amazed upon hearing it. “Oh, haha, thank you Samaira, I will write something for you too, okay?”

“Haha, really, wow, I would love it.”

They didn’t read the other poetry as they knew the complexity of his words, and the feeling behind them, they left it as they respect the feelings, it was quite personal, but now, what was personal for him was the same for Nasia. The bus arrived, and the sisters boarded it, while Arav waited for another, cause of the route difference.

“We are meeting tomorrow, yeah?” said Samaira. “Oh yeah, we will be meeting tomorrow for sure.”

“Yes, you better come as Aria will be coming too, okay?” “Oh sure, haha, it’s been some time since I met her.” Samaira gave him a hug and Nasia gave him a kiss, saying, “Bye love, till tomorrow.”

They reached home while talking about him all the way, and nothing bothered them much, but the seriousness of his condition. Where he reached his home, thinking about Grace. He wondered why every time he felt happy, something always came his way to show him where he stood, beneath the ground, where he must feel small. He took a shower to be light headed and to forget the black eyes of the red feelings of Grace, the one who was like hung wind, now free in her own will, to be confined no more. He Dropped a text to Nasia about the day and asked her to call him to before he went to sleep, lightening his head as much as possible to sleep.

When the morning light hit him, and a knock on the door, he woke up, blind in the bright light, thinking who could be at his door, went to opened the door, there was a parcel man, who gave him a parcel from the same publishing house. He opened the letter and read what was in there, he found a pen, a pen? and the instructions to send them the poems according to him, as they would appreciate his words anyway, in his way. Feeling the morning colours after long, he felt so beautiful and started writing pieces for them, after being done with his daily morning routine, breakfast, shower and then coffee. In the meantime, Nasia called him to tell him not to go anywhere, but just be ready, as they had planned to come to a place near his house, 'Brew-souls cafe', to have some good coffee there.

They decided to get to his roots by getting into his phone, he didn't mind anyone taking his phone, but they didn't want to let him know that they were trying to find something in it. When Aria reached there, she happily reunited with Samaira. "See you, bitch, your sister is so amazing, I love her more than you, haha." "Oh ohkay, then tell your love to take all your art stuff you asked me to buy, I'll give it back to them, then."

"Oh, clever, haha, no I love you too, haha, but till the time I get my stuff. Clever me." Aria was precious for them as she was best friends with both.

When they left to meet him, they made a sort of a plan to get into his phone, in order to find something helpful. Aria being unaware of what was happening with them, tried to cope up, at least she knew somethings about him, through Nasia, obviously. It was Aria who could help Nasia, as she was meeting him after days. "You two will talk surely, and in that time, I will take his phone and see if I can get something," Nasia said.

He had been waiting for them outside the cafe, just looking at the colours of the leafs and birds there on a branch from where the leafs were falling, reminding him of an ideology from an Indian Myth, of a pigeon in the Himalayas of Lord Shiva. He tried to remember the theory of moksha when someone's hands covered his eyes. He didn't panic at all this time, as he knew who could be doing this. "Tell the name of mine, if you may!" The touch was different, it was not the muse to his words, who could it be? "Umm…Samaira, haha?"

She hit the back of his head in disappointment. "Look at my face, am I?" "Oh Aria, wow, how are you? Haha. Sorry dear, I was so confused. Her long hair fell on his face while she hugged him. "At least you were right in guessing that it was not she, haha." His level of joy increased on seeing Aria and them together after so long, when Samaira guessed that he, Arav, must have had his coffee in the morning, so he might not take another one here, to which Nasia responded, "No, that's your biggest misconception regarding him, this loser, haha." Aria said, "Yeah, he might leave me, but not his coffee." "Nasia, no, haha, I can't leave you for you are my coffee," Arav said. "What? Haha, that was so beautiful," said Samaira and Aria together. Naisa blushed, looking at him. While at the same time, she thought about him and his roots and what she might find in his phone. They went to the cafe, took a seat, Aria claimed that she was meeting him and Samaira after long, so she was going to give them a coffee treat, she asked them what they would like to have.

As they had planned earlier, it happened so naturally by itself, that they didn't need to create any distraction or plan an execution like detectives. Arav reached for his wallet but Aria, refused to let him pay as it had been a treat from her. He left his phone on the table, and when they left, Nasia unlocked his phone to see if she could get something. It was inapt to do so, but she knew that she was doing well. Scaling his phone from notes to photos, there were not much photos there though, so she decided to go to his contacts, useful, might be.

"So Arav, what's up with your writing thing, it's been some time, yeah?" "Yeah, true, oh that reminds me, this publisher..." He told her almost everything, how his writing was going, about the journals and the publishers. She was so elated to know that they were now together, even by not saying it or showing it directly, but it so obvious to everyone. Arav told her about the Paris thing that Samaira had done for them, and when he asked her to come with them, he really meant it. "Haha, I wish, dear, I wish, but I really got a lot of work. Samaira did ask me before she made the bookings, but I can't. As Nasia would not be here, I have to handle her stuff too, and some important meetings with some art collectors are coming up, so."

"Ah, yeah I get it, next time then, you must take a trip with us, soon." They talked about almost everything that had taken place in the last few days and Aria told him about her work too, and wishes him good-luck for the publishing thing. After spending enough time with him in a manner to allow Nasia to do her work, they went back to their table.

Nasia had long been done with his phone, and the sisters were talking when they came back, for a moment, Aria thought that nothing had happened, but she knew the will of Nasia, and that she would have done something. He told them about the publishing thing from that morning, and shared some jokes while they had their coffee, and Aria teasing the couple about their Paris trip, and how lucky Nasia was to have him and a sister like Samaira, and how she could attend the art fair there, which would be beneficial for both Aria and Nasia, she also gave them some tips on love making, being in the city of love, in order to pull their legs. After an hour and a half, having spent some quality time together, they decided to leave. "Meet me soon, okay? It felt so great to meet a pure soul like you," Aria said, and he remarked the same in return. "Write them as truth," said Nasia, and they kissed before departing. The charm on Samaira was of true glow, but she seemed vague to him, Aria didn't know what had taken place behind their backs, but she was happy anyway.

After he left, Aria asked if they had got something or not. "Yeah, and it's of great turn, dear." When she asked what it was, she said, "Okay, so I found the contact of someone named 'Nash', and in the contact description, it was written, 'Liar of Fate, don't contact'. I don't know what that really means, or if the contact is real or not, but I am worried for him."

"How did you know that it would be the only useful contact, it must have just been a name in the contact, right?" Samaira asked. "That's what the thing is, baby. The 'H' and the starting letter 'N' in the name was in capital, that's what made this contact an interesting one, and when I opened the description, it was the only contact with such a description." "Oh, that needs a state of zone, glad you have it, haha," Aria said.

When Samaira and Aria asked her if she was going to call the number, not being sure who the person was, or if the contact really existed, considering the past experience with Anvisha, she said, “Yeah, but whatever it is, it must be a helpful one, I’ll call him in a while, after reaching home.”

Arav, back at his home, was feeling so glad to have met Aria again, not to mention Nasia and her sister too, he went back to writing after a while, starting with the pieces, as he was unrestricted to write about anything, he started with the truth of the truth. Nasia, on the other hand, made a call to the one she had got the number of from his contacts, while Samaira and Aria went to get some stuff for home decor for Nasia.

Not thinking what she was going to ask him, she just made the call. The phone kept ringing, no one answered, she attempted a second time, again, no ne answered the call, she wondered if it was even a real contact, she left the phone, downcast, and lay down on the couch, holding her head, giving herself a massage, closed her eyes, took a power nap, when she heard her phone ringing after about half an hour. Frowning, with her heart rate increased, she saw that it was a call from the same number, she picked it up within four rings.

“Hello? Who’s this?” sounded a voice, modulated, yet heavy, as if coming directly from the throat.

“Hi, Nash?” she confirmed beforehand.

“Yeah, may I know who it is?”

“Sir, I am Nasia, I contacted you regarding a person you may know, I found your contact in his phone, thinking it might helpful for his condition.” “Oh, okay, what’s the patient’s name? Is he mine?”

"Yeah sir, he is. Arav is the name. Do... do you know him?" she said.

"Wait," he recalled his name a few times. "Oh, Arav, damn, how could I forget about this son of god with the ability to write words of pure, but he hasn't showed up in a really long time, I was his Psychiatrist back then, I have been concerning about him, but he got busy with others, he stopped seeing me, blocked me from his contacts, who are you? How you know him?"

She felt so relieved to know that he knew him, he had been his psychiatrist too, finally something effective she could do for him, thinking if she should claim herself as his girlfriend or a friend. "Wow, you know him, yes, I am so relieved, God, I am his girlfriend, and have been worrying about him so much lately, I think he is with some elements of his imagination still, a friend of his. But why did he stop seeing you? Was there something you remarked that he didn't like? And what's the problem with him, I want to treat him for real."

"Ah, that delicate spirit finally made a friend, and that too a girlfriend, I am glad to know that, really," he said in excitement. "Oh, he is still with her? That's not so good now, that might fail his receptors of responding, I don't know, dear Nasia, it's just that she had heavily been sitting on his mind when I tried to make him encounter the reality, for some days it worked, but later, he adopted some other, and made another friend in the state of being hurt to know that Manik was not real, I still remember that name, and later some girl came, what was it, umm..." he couldn't remember her name. "Is it Anvisha?" "Oh yes, that, Anvisha, is he still with her? shit."

She got more tensed on hearing these words, but she knew that she could treat him, and she would, she had made a commitment to herself, for the sake of her love. “Oh, I want to treat him sir, could you please help me?” She knew how serious this was for both of them. “Sure, I would like to guide you, for I know, he won’t see me, and don’t let him know about all this, this might cause him some major depression and hysteria. Let’s talk in person, meet me if you can, day after tomorrow, at my clinic.”

“I would appreciate any help from you, as you were his psychiatrist, and obviously know how to deal with him, I can’t wait to meet you, if you don’t mind sir, can we meet now, I mean today, please?” she didn’t know if it was right for her to ask him this. “Oh my dear, the crave of love, I can understand that, umm, I will need to cancel a date with my wife then, okay, don’t come to my clinic then, as it’s a off today. What about near Borough market? There’s a good place near the park where we can sit and discuss.”

“Oh sure, yeah, I really appreciate it sir, and sorry for your date, really.” She was a bit embarrassed but she had no time to wait. “Oh don’t be, I can see that thirst, and why would I not be glad to treat a foregone patient of mine, at 1:30, okay? So that I can spare time for my wife in the evening, if you don’t mind?”

“Oh, sure, it’s perfect, it’s 12:30 right now, I’ll be there sir, thank you, yeah, wife is important too, haha.” “Okay, haha right, a happy life with a happy wife, meet you then.”

Nasia was nervous, she couldn’t think of anything, totally blank, zoned out, as she knew he was busy writing today, she could meet his doctor today itself and he wouldn’t come to know about it, she was ready in time. Before leaving, she called up Samaira to let them know about this doctor she had found, and that she was going to meet him and would be late. She was in such a hurry, she left her home in great hassle.

Reaching there before time showed her care towards Arav, she waited near the park, sitting on a public bench, it was not at all crowded, 'Nash knows about the place well, as to keep things secret, oh, obviously he is a psychiatrist,' she guffawed to herself. At sharp 1:30, Nash called her to see if she was there. "Oh yeah, I am sitting on this bench right in front of the park, near the market."

"Yeah, I see you, you are in a blue jacket, right?" –"Oh yeah, that's right."

She turned to see where he was and noticed a man in a casual suit walking towards her, she knew it was him, tall, a sharp jaw, and yes, he was smart too. She noticed a bag in his hand, perhaps with something related to his work, or perhaps he was coming from some sort of a meeting. "Nasia, yeah?" he approached her and asked in a gentle and calm tone. "Yeah, sir." They shook hands and he took a seat beside her on the bench, the same one where she had been waiting for him earlier.

They started with a formal talk first, he asked her what she did, and where they had met. Then she told him everything about what she had noticed about him, and what was going with him those days. It was clear from the doctor's face, that he was really concerned and wanted to help his former patient who had stopped seeing him because he was disturbed by him. He opened his bag and took a file out with 'Arav' written in bold on it. 'Oh, it is his file, great,' she exclaimed within.

"It's a hypothesis I made on him two days before he stopped coming by, you might not understand everything that is written in this," he opened the file without making any eye contact with her, "But I brought it with me to tell you to look out for some of his tendencies."

Nash told her everything about his condition, how his defence mechanism had stopped working, and his cognitive and behavioural nature in the most simple language that she could understand. When she asked who Manik was, he said, "He was a friend of his during his schizophrenic period, but when he encountered the fact that he was not real, it caused him great stress that his senses and traits were changing so casually. After a period, he befriended her, Anvisha, but her grip on his health was so tight that he couldn't handle it and his conscience instructed him to stop seeing me." He told her that Arav was aware of everything, but kept in his unconscious mind. "I did not get enough time to treat him with several therapies like psychoanalytic, classical, operant conditioning and more. He used to show a schizoid personality, actually the disorders of motor behaviour. I couldn't really reach the exact problem that was co-occurring again and again that was causing the Post-traumatic disorder, because he left so early. I wish I could have done more, or maybe I became a bit selfish for my own theory, that's the guilt I have though."

She was listening to everything but when he mentioned 'guilt', it really caught her attention. "What is it?" she asked. "It was not one thing, there were several problems he dealt with that caused him this, if at one time he is showing the traits of Obsessive Compulsive Disorder, the other moment he showed abnormal behaviour while being touched, that is Haphephobia. The thing is, it was not Bipolar Personality

Disorder, but something new that I tried to give a name to. I personally call it a reversal state of personality and psychology, with the association of learning and failed positive cognition, where some traits of Neuroticism are always there. Reversal schizophrenia, I call it at times, as he saw her imagination and voices, which had the problem with their voices and imagination."

He gave her the ways be which she could treat him in a pattern, and motivated her enough telling her everything that she could do for him. Just before leaving, he said that Arav had a diary at home, that only he knew about besides Arav. "He can't open the diary as it has things about Manik and Anvisha that he wrote by himself, but it can motivate him to get over his problem. Get that diary somehow, it's an easy gateway to treat him, if he reads it one, he will surely recall his past time with me and the nature of his condition, by seeing the things that he wrote in his own way and language, that's called coping by self. It might be emotional, appraisal focussed coping. He will surely come up with his own defence mechanism, that will lead him to his stream of consciousness, and this mechanism will block the way of all possible anxiety, depression, panic attacks or PTSD (post-traumatic stress disorder)." To this she asked, "How do we prevent him from lending himself to negativism?"

"Since you have become his strength, motivation, and a type of reinforcement, he has accepted you as his own part. His conscious mind might not allow you to destroy Anvisha and treat him, but everything else has ceased in his unconscious mind, and you will act like a psychoanalytic therapy, entering into his cognitive mind and affect the response receptors of his senses. Keep it in mind, however, to be very careful, attempt this in the very level of ecstasy in him, where you have captured his sane with you, in the perfect environment, and his stimuli will act accordingly."

After about five minutes more of talk, when he had completed and directed her to the conclusion, he told her to be in regular touch with him. He said, "I will always be there to help him in any possible way and to meet him when he comes to his own real life." She thanked him, as she now had everything she needed for him. After this, the doctor left. On the way back home, she recalled everything, the doctor's advice, and thought of getting his diary that was still there in his shelf. She hadn't noticed it when she had been at his house earlier. She knew how to do it though, and when. She decided to get the next day, as she knew he wouldn't notice its absence, for he was caught up in time management then, by writing and stuff.

Nasia told everything to Samaira and Aria, and they understood the complexity of his condition, and recommend her in her distress and nervousness of how to make him encounter his own diary, the best and easiest way for him to be alright. "Paris, we are going there, what would be a more perfect environment, right?" "Oh yeah, how could I forget about that? Paris would be the best of the best setting for this." She felt relieved about everything, at least for a while, and started planning on how to get his diary. Samaira left for something related to her work after a while, leaving Aria and Nasia at home. They went to sleep on the couch, cuddling like a couple. Aria knew how to make her feel unlatched from her distress, and decided to stay with them that night.

Nasia couldn't stop thinking about Arav even in her sleep, while Arav fell asleep whilst writing some of his pieces, unknowing of what was happening for him.

The next morning, Aria and Nasia went to his place to get his diary before it got too late, and so that she could read what was there to share, as they had to leave for Paris in a few days. They made their appearance there, with the pretext of going shopping to get some cool clothes. Before leaving his home, Nasia and Aria asked Arav to change out of the shirt he was wearing, to wear something more bright. "But it's a beautiful shirt, what's wrong in it? And you liked it earlier," he said. Nasia was trapped, but she said, "Haha, of course it's beautiful, but I just want to see you in something more bright." "Oh, that way, haha okay, a minute please." He went to change his shirt in the room. In the mean time, she rushed over to the shelf and found his diary finally, and placed it in Aria's bag. It was all normal when he came out, having changed his shirt. They left for shopping at a nearby street and came back home in the evening.

Back home, Nasia, along with Samaira and Aria, started going through the diary, worn out but not too old, as it had been at the top and sometimes under the shelf all this while. She opened it and read all that Arav had written, starting from describing the good days, then Manik, and then the story of Anvisha, it was as if his life's saga had been written down. Pages after pages, it showed that he knew everything about himself, but was just hiding from it. "Then the facts started to hit me, and I know my problem now, Nash told me everything, I think he is a liar, he is implementing all of his theories on me, but I believe in him too. So, I have decided not to see him and to keep up with Anvisha, for Manik died a long time ago, and she was the one standing with me through that bad time."

They got emotional while reading it, as they now knew everything about him. "So this Paris trip is our last and best hope now," Samaira said. Now that they knew his secret, a secret to be kept, like it had been earlier; they made the commitment to treat him for real, as they were the only ones who know about him.

Days pass by, and the Paris trip drew closer. Arav had been writing for his publisher, and being done with his pieces, he was a free mind now, to be on this trip, which was an opportunity for him to be full of life, and for them to strike him with reality. He recited some of his words, a micro-poetry, in despair that Anvisha was not talking to him, and he didn't know the reason, they knew what was happening, however. His unconscious mind was becoming stronger than his conscious made up of fibs, because of Nasia, who was becoming the power of truth for him.

In the may world, why you not?

Waiting forever, to be the fact, I caught.

The words I want, I end up saying to myself

As time changes, someone is changing in Stranger

and my words, my world, and her my boundless bird.

Chapter Eight

Let us go home, for the evening asks to be risen again, not to be forgotten in the mist, but to remember. For some, it is a new era of the sky to be fallen in the middle of the top of a hill, while for some, it is the foregone beginning that had never begun; a saga that had never unfolded. What a charm they had, a glow of purity was shining in their eyes, Samaira was happy for her sister but worried at the same time as she had to be, by making Arav encounter with reality, risking to lose her own sanity by indulging in something that might not be a lifelong possibility, any serious incident could occur, and boom, he would be gone, again, what then? But she knew, whatever Nasia was doing, was in her senses, and she would have supported her anyway.

With a relaxed mind and nerves, Arav said, "if you ask me to write Paris down, I might fail, ask me to write of Paris' romantics, and watch me create miracles of love", while taking a deep breath to inhale the alien air. It was cold there, Samaira had left for her meeting an hour after they had reached the hotel, leaving them in their room. "And if you ask me to paint the romantics down, I might fail, but ask me to print them on the canvas for a realistic romanticism of love and pain," Nasia said, having borrowed Arav's tongue, as she often did now. "Whoa! An artist tasting the tongue of words again, beautiful, and I would love to create a destruction out of your piece and mine, by indulging them into a new period of ours."

She was with him totally, but not wholly, as she had been thinking about how to make it happen all this time. She said, "Hey, baby, there's an Art fair here day after tomorrow, and it's going to be huge. Let's go there, what say?" She thought that she might get a change to get into his creative destructive mind full of words and thoughts after the fair. "Why not, haha, we'll go there, if you want to."

Scaling the streets of Paris, for that time before the fair, all she wanted was just to be in his arms, to feel the new world with him, with the one she wanted to stay with for a lifetime. They spent their time holding hands, jumping around, and making fun of themselves. All of a sudden, it looked like it was about to rain, and they felt as if some music had come alive in them, the music that only they could hear, and they rushed to some random cafe and bakery to get shelter and some food too, and told Samaira to catch them there itself. "I'll be there in a while, order for yourselves till then."

Coffee was must, then a salad and a mushroom sandwich soon followed, while they found themselves lost again and again in each other's eyes they could touch it, talking down the universe, the beauty of an arrow that hurts but the love it causes is even greater. For a change, he was not like he had been earlier, lost all the time, it was her, Nasia, the reality, not the same as Anvisha, but as real as the lie he was living. She wanted to hold him, as hard as stone, as soft as a petal, remembering the time they had made love, while he was doing the same, lost in her eyes, not saying a word, when Samaira came and sat next to them, not disturbing them, all the surrounding voices and sights had dissolved in the background, it was just their eyes and the zoned out silence.

She didn't disturb them, went to order for herself and then came back and said, "I think the impact of Paris' breeze has been quite strong on you both asses." Her words shocked them back into reality and Nasia said, "When did you come?" "Oh? As if you care about it, bitch, I have ordered myself food too, and have been looking at you both for a couple of minutes now." "Haha, no, it's not like that, it's your sister who took me away with her, to a world full of fairies, where they were real." "Oh, look at you baby, haha, beautiful words, bless you both."

She told them about her meeting, and asked them what they want to do for the rest of the day, and decided to go on a ride as she had got a car from her colleagues as a welcome present to explore places in the city. After being done with their food, they soon left. She, Nasia, decides to be wholly with him, for at least the time till they made him encounter reality. Taking a trip back, Manik to Anvisha, she talked herself down, she knew, it was her voice that could calm the storms of an ocean in just a blink for Arav.

Exploring Paris, they decided to not go to the Eiffel Tower that day; keeping it for the next day, before the Art fair there. After a full day of travelling to exploring, they returned back to the hotel terribly tired. Samaira had given them a separate room to be comfortable by themselves, but they still chose to be with Samaira till late in the night, eating pizza, sharing laughter, cracking jokes, a gesture of pure love towards Samaira, which was what she wholly deserved. At two in the morning they left her room, as she had another meeting to attend early that morning.

It was so different this time, when they left for their room, even a simple touch of their skin felt so sensational, she ran her fingers through his, he was still looking at her and her lips, like she did. A smile conveyed the obvious, to commit the sin of love again, but this time, a pure form of it, full of it, like the body of an angel to be scaled like the mountain. Entering the room, they locked the door and stood there, all smiles had gone now, it was there but not on their faces, far from the world, form the voices around, with nothing but the sound of their hearbeats, hand in hand, eye in eye, no words, still as time, and waiting to be in the sin as time.

Not saying a word, not even a single one, they wanted to, but couldn't, as they let the silence scream between them, Nasia leaned in to him, closing her eyes. "Let the fall in your arms take place for a lifetime", she said it as a whisper. "May I not embrace you, for I have captured the soul in me." He couldn't wait to let her unheard soul land in her, within her, he held her head, and by her neck, removed a portion of her hair from right to left to get to her ears, he kissed her there, and she did the same, taking her hand over his back and the other on his neck, it was going to be as hard as the fall of autumn.

Reaching to each other's lips and starting it as it ends to every beginning to taste and relish the marrow of time caught on their lips. Form her curves to his edges, from her heart to the beats, they were so in the moment, moving towards the bed while still kissing, more passionate this time, she was flying with the wind, while he had gone like the wind. Taking down the touch every time, they touched their lips to the body, she bit his neck again, going hard on him, oh, the sin was committing itself, vicariously. They knew where it would go next.

From the subtle moment, to the sharply passionate, she bit his neck again, and he pulled her by her hair to kiss her from her neck to her belly, taking out her shirt, as she did the same, a bit hurriedly, she arched her back on his hand, that had gripped her like his coffee, and he tasted the caffeine on her body by kissing her from her lips to her neck, then her breast to feel the shakes of her belly. Nasia nearly scratched his back, being more arched, he put his finger in her mouth, and she licked it like the time, wrapping within themselves, he grabbed her by the back of her neck again, for a moment to enjoy the sight of her, and when she sat over him on her knees, standing bigger than him, pushing him back by his forehead, she went into a zone of lust, of love, to be loved by the era of passionate making of it.

In the blanket of sin, she moaned his name and Arav did the same when she was being hard on him, taking a lead on him. "Uhh, make the crime of love," she said with a heavy breath, "Arav," so smoothly and it become as subtle as it had been hard earlier. With breaths of being loved and the taste that had lingered, bites on the neck, scratches on the back, they had been so in it, perhaps like Leda and the Swan, no, like an Artist and a Writer. All naked, taking the time on their tongues as they rolled it over the other's body, with the clock they slept, naked in the blanket with each other.

Waking up to Samaira's phone call, she found it even more cold than the day before. While he still lay asleep, she casually turned to him, kissed his forehead. Samaira said on the phone, "Dear, wake up. We'll be going sight-seeing today. There is some other stuff too, I have to tell you something, I think it would be great, i am coming to your room in five." "Oh. Okay, yeah," Nasia replied in a sleepy voice.

She put on a bathrobe, feeling too lazy to wear clothes, and opened the door before-hand, so as not to let the door bell disturb him. "Morning, dear," Samaira said, as she entered in her formal clothes. "Morning, done with the meeting, I guess?" Nasia asked. "Yeah."

"So where will we be going?" she asked in a cracking sleepy voice.

"Ah, yeah, places, haha, some great places, and then the Eiffel Tower for dinner."

"Wait, wasn't that for tomorrow, and for dinner? You okay, Samaira?" she asked totally confused.

"Haha, yeah, obviously. I have booked a table at the Eifel Tower, at the top of it, and I thought wouldn't it be great to show him that diary finally, huh? First, it's so beautiful there, and the vibes are so pure, secondly, we will be going to the top of it for dinner, just us."

"Yeah, you are right, but you didn't have to do such a fancy thing. Really, why did you book it, Samaira?" She hugged her, with a rush of ecstasy and love for her too.

"Haha, yeah, it's just me being your elder sister maybe, haha, no need to thank me," she paused for a while, "Oh God, look, look, whoa!" "What, what happened?"

"What's that for?" Samaira asked, pointing to her neck. "Is that a scar? Ahh, seems something like that, maybe the writer tried to write a poem on you," Samaira mocked. Nasia was so embarrassed for a while, but a moment later it felt beautiful to her.

"Haha, yeah, fuck, you saw it, haha, God, go now, I am going to wake him up." "Yeah, get ready in an hour, maybe, I will be in my room."

Pulling her thoughts away from her love bite to the thought of how to do it, with the diary, she told herself that she was brave enough to solve it out on her own, and to not stress over it too much, as it was just the moment that mattered there, and in that moment, his inner self would be so calm and that calmness will get him through it all. She woke him up, kissing him, and asked him to get ready, as they had not come there to sleep. When she left for a bath after a while, he said, "Hey, wait," getting up from the bed. "Ah, let's shower together."

"Whoa, a writer getting naughty, haha, yeah, it'll be beautiful," she replied, looking at him, oh the love was not going down, but this time, it was just a shower. He got up and followed her into the bathroom.

They met with Samaira at noon. She started laughing as soon as she saw them and said, "Wait, haha, I thought it was just the writer who tried to write on her, but it's the artist too, who tried to paint."

For a while, he didn't get it, but when Nasia said, "Stop it, haha, oh shit, Samaira," he figured what was she was talking about and hid behind Nasia shyly. "Yeah, your sister is too much to handle, haha."

They left soon to explore Paris, breaking laughter, glad that it was not raining anymore, hopping on to places, random streets, tourist attractions, etc. It was going perfectly well, Nasia was not even thinking about how she was going to do what she wanted to, but she was confident within that since she was with him, he wouldn't go through any panic attacks for as long as she'd be standing with him. Stepping into a cafe to have breakfast at lunch time, they found it all blue, the blood running in him was all blue, when he spotted an old man standing near the cafe, observing everyone, as if he was the same old man who waited around to help others, but he was not. He then told the two of them about the old man, the story of how he had helped him, and for an instant they thought that it might be another one of his unconscious creatinos, but it sounded so real, that Nasia felt it.

Sometimes, there's nothing but a sudden urge to ask, ask all the questions from the age of childhood that never got answered, like a tree, that took years and years to grow big, standing stiff, unmovable, yet moving with the surrounding. She observed him all through the day, while they were on their way to different places, that sudden urge to cry was crying in her, she looked at the diary in her bag, and then at him, thinking how he would react, or if she even had to do it, getting no thoughts but the one worrying her the most, would it be a good decision?

She asked him if he believed in her, and an expected reply came back, but what she felt in her was a betrayal, that this brainstorming had to happen, to break him and to make him himself again. She didn't ask any further but just smiled, Arav thought for a second as to why she had even asked it, but the next moment he let it go. They were about to reach the Tower, and she got more and more nervous with time, while Samaira was just worried about him, thinking if it would break Arav or Nasia, but it didn't need to break, for it was meant to construct a whole new life.

When they got off the car, walking towards the destiny, from where they could either take a flight to Neverland, or land at a no-surface area, he looked on astonished to see the beauty, the beauty of Paris, while she saw him, just him. "What hands made this beauty of so many stories, a world of its own," he said, while looking at the ambience and experiencing the moment there, but she still continued to look oddly at him, she tried not to, but it was in her, deep within, rushing and shivering, like a body standing still under a frozen lake.

"Yeah, it is. Hey Arav, you really do believe in me right? Like, with whatever I do?" Nasia asked again. Samaira looked at her with pity in her eyes, but that was the moment to be. "Nasia, are you alright? You know, I will. Even through the worst storms, I will. Why do you look so worried? Tell me."

"Oh, it's nothing, really, just my heart for you, " she said, her eyes locked with his, "I know you will."

When the night had finally arrived, for the bespoke truth to come out, the truth that had laid hidden in him for years, she was feeling nervous, but was pulled up by the fact that she was with him and that she wouldn't let anything inapt take place. Samaira was a bit worried too, she glanced at the diary in the bag and took a deep breath. While going up to the top of the Tower, he felt the rush of adrenaline, and thanked Samaira again for having sponsored their trip and for surprises like that.

A red carpet, piped-in music, a big table with three chairs, fancy as antique, a view to die for, everything suddenly seemed so small from that height, but not the love that he was with, which only seemed to grow bigger and bigger with every moment, yet there was something, some part of his feeling that asked him to stay on the ground for it could mess with his mind, but when he looked at her in that unease, all of it evaporated, just the look of her, and her words were his saviours, for he was still alive maybe, not thinking about anything else, just sitting next to her, sharing in the universe of their thoughts, but when the dessert arrived after the food, the air of pleasure suddenly turned into a breathe of tension and anxiety.

"Arav, you believe in me right?" she asked again.

"Nasia, it's the third time you are asking me this, just tell me what is it now, from the very moment we arrived here, you seem so nervous and zoned out, baby, tell me, please?"

She looked at Samaira, who nodded in return. She then turned back to look at him, smiling pitifully, and collected enough courage to say, "You are not allowed to speak a word till I finish. I'll answer every question of yours in time." He sat still, but he wouldn't be there for long.

"I know it will be hard, baby, but guess what? I am with you, you know that," she said, to remind him that she had always been there when he needed someone the most, to gain his unconscious trust in her. "It's all about you, not us, and no matter what, we'll always be standing right beside you, not out of sympathy but empathy." She stood up from her chair and placed her hand on his shoulder, maintaining eye contact. He stood up too. "It is about the things that have been going on with you, for years."

He couldn't take it anymore, something rushed up in his blood. Breathing heavily, so as not to lose his breath, and also suffocating a bit, he said, "What is it, Nasia? You are making me anxious, seriously, what, tell me quickly." "Oh, how I wish I could, but I need to gain a pace slowly." Taking a deep breath, she asked him about Doctor Nash.

On hearing his name first, it sounded to him like a stranger's, but after a second, he said, "What? What did you say?" stammering, as if the foregone trauma had come back to hit him hard. "Nash, how the fuck do you know him? Nash, a fucking liar Nash, a doctor of killing, Nash, is he the one?" he asked, his voice rising in pitch with every word. She nodded, not reacting much, but controlling her tears from falling down. "How the hell do you know about him, and why would you even fucking ask me about this dumbf? What about him?" It was so clear that his conscious mind was being terribly hard on him, sitting on him, controlling him to be as harsh as he could, but he couldn't, not when she was standing before him.

“Arav, look at me,” she said loudly, trying to control him, holding him by his face, “I told you not to speak a word until I finish, don’t you get this?” Nasia was being a bit harsh on him, but that’s what she felt was right at that moment. She didn’t want to do it at all, it hurt her to do it, but not more than it hurt him. He said, “Yeah, sorry.”

“He is not a liar, your sanely kept thoughts are. Your brain is playing with you, baby, and I won’t let that happen, listen to me, you said you believe in me, right? Why would I try to destruct you with lies then? Answer me?” “No, you are here to save me.” He knew it, but found it so hard to deal with, yet he had to. “Nash is a good man, okay? Not that bad, if not good, okay? He was only trying to help you, and fuck him, forget about the man, okay? If you don’t want to recall him, don’t. You will surely understand everything in a while,” she said and pulled out the diary from her bag. PTSD (Post Traumatic Stress Disorder) started building in him, strangulating for something more, she hugged him tight to keep a hold over him. The breeze, the cold breeze and view was so perfect behind, to outdo even the truth. Even if he got the anxiety, it would have gone away by the serenity of their surrounding, that’s what his brain was dealing with, uncertain of how to react.

“Manik, Anvisha,” she said and then stopped to see his reaction, but he was numb, senseless, as if his response receptors had gone down. She held him tight, and said, “Stay with me, don’t let the voices in your head hit you, look in my eyes, baby.” He noded.

At this stage, she didn’t feel like saying anything anymore, but that had been enough for him to recall, and she let him be, he fell on his knees, numb, alien to his surroundings and even to himself, she let him, but after a moment, when he went deep into his sane, she took out the diary and offered it to him to take it. On seeing that diary, he struggled hard to be there with them, he could feel a panic attack rising, but before it could get any worse, she took a hold on him, sat on the ground next to him, and offered him the diary.

The diary, that he feared the most, was there in front of him, he brushed his fingers over it, the pages, the smell, everything, a threatening black out, but she wouldn't let that happen, she shook his head, "No, you have to stay, if not for yourself, for me, take it, open it, move your sight over it." As he opened it, shivering, as if a storm had arrived, eyes red, tears falling constantly, but he held her hand so tight, it hurted her, she looked at Samaira, their tears drop too, but she could not react to the pain he was giving her. Recalling all the foregone memories, re-reading the thing he had written, recognising his own hand-writing, feeling it as if it was engraved.

As he read his words, all the voices in his head started telling him to close the book and throw it away, but the vibes he was getting from holding Nasia's hand, were stronger than these voices. He read as if he was revising a chapter he had read several times before, page after page after page, turning and turning, smiling and crying, when he read it was nothing, they didn't exist, neither Manik nor Anvisha, he read and read, took his time, and threw the diary away, got up, loosening the grip on her, she let him, she knew he had had his encounter with the reality, the thing they had been dreading.

He walked away from them, looking at the view, but it was not the view that he was hailing at all, it was himself, he tried hard to find himself, he felt the wind laughing at him, he looked back, found everyone else laughing at him, there were a lot of people, but Nasia just kept looking at him, expressionless, he tried to gain his consciousness again, slapped himself, screamed, "You are here, your voices are the hate." Screaming:

Oh the aura of might,

exit if you exist,

I am stronger than the powers of your hate

and as light as your prays.

How could it be, everything came up right in front of the sightless sight? She ran towards him to get a hold on him, just by holding his hand, she knew that the touch of a loved one was enough to stop the storming brain, he gained his sight again, living different settings, moment after moment. He saw Manik, then Anvisha, then Nash, then some random places he was drowning at, a hill top he saw himself jumping from, but the her touch reacted with him as a silver-cord, she held onto him, trying to get into his head.

Lies, lies, he screamed within, saying to himself, it had all been lies, recalling the moments when he craved for Anvisha and she was not there, when he had asked Manik to help him, and he was not there, recalling his own words from the diary that they didn't exist, "You are the real one, only you, don't let the psychic of imagination of destruction hit you, you are the one." Remembering the words of the old man, every word of his about life, about sanity, about love, about thoughts and the brain which played with us every time for its own entertainment, it was his choice if he wanted to become a game for his own brain.

He laughed, and then cried, sometimes screamed, sometimes whispered, but wouldn't let the voices occur to him again.

You never been there
every moment I lived a night-mare
the night mare of your dare
to die, but I grew in stronger creature
not the hell you, I am my own teacher
with the classes of nature and surround
no one can bind the unbound bound.

He repeated this moment by moment, then collapsed, collapsing in himself, he was about to faint, when Samaira rushed to him and splashed water on his face to get him back there with them, he looked at Nasia, a blurry sight, and tears kept pouring down his face.

He weeped the guts out of him, all emotions, all the suppressed cries, his unconscious mind was now coming to life, he tried to convince himself that he was real, and the ones he was with right that moment, her jacket was all drenched with his tears now, and she cried too, but Samaira assured her by telling her, “No Nasia, you can’t, for you are the only strength he is left with.” He cried and cried in her lap, and Samaira held onto Nasia. He, couldn’t get anything to his sane mind, as if his cognition was about to be released with his breath, and she was with him, holding him as he always held his coffee, “Now that you’re here, baby, now you are, between us, to your fullest.” He heard her, but not the words, just her, in his blurred sight, she was the only one focused, he closed his eyes, they called him back, but he had gone to sleep, swooning, lost his balance of consciousness, but after some minutes, his nerves regained and his pulse came back to normal .

They left after he found his balance, not talking the whole way back to the hotel, neither talking to himself, he was seeing but not observing, benumbed, listening hard to the voices that were not there with him anymore, he looked at her, she already had her eyes on him, the eyes of his beloved. He said, "I might not say it, I know, I want to, but it's not coming from within, but thank you for saving me." Nasia put her finger on his lips to keep him shush, she didn't want to get special appreciation for this, as she has done it for herself, for her love. There being not much conversation between them, Samaira went to her room, after leaving them in theirs. She kissed his forehead before leaving and said to her, "I am proud of my younger mirror."

As soon as he lay down on the bed, he went into deep sleep, while Nasia had her eyes on him all night. Even in his sleep, he was not there, but more with himself, embracing himself after ages, cutting through the web of his own mental games on him, he was there, livelier than ever, looking at the falls and diving into them, but that night, there, he did not drown, he had learnt to swim, when he jumped from the cliff, he did not fall, but was flying his way down. When the deserts came, there were no cactii, but only daffodils, and when he looked down, he found himself up in the sky, in the rainbow, as if the powers of spirituality were being showered on him, yes, as he was back to his own originality, he slept, not with the frowns, but with the factuality of his own being, as calm as the same old feather.

When she woke up the next morning, as she had fell asleep while looking at him the whole night, she saw something strange, he was already awake before her, and was writing something on the hotel pad, he looked at her, smiled, got up and kissed her, asking, "Do you want a coffee?" "Arav, are you alright?" Uncertain if she had to ask this, but waking up to see this was a bit worrying for her, as she thought that he had lost his sane, as a person could after a heavy breakdown, but it wasn't like that at all. "Haha, you crazy? I was writing something and let you asleep, I didn't want to wake you up, you must have been very tired after last night."

"Oh, what?" she said, still trying to believe it, "Will you show me what you are writing?" "Oh, haha, look at you, you are still not awake, your voice is still as asleep as you were, glossed eyes, I can see, go and wash your face, get refreshed and I'll show you, I am yet to completing it, baby, and I have already ordered coffee for both of us, haha."

He was back to himself, he was alive, for his breath that he felt and inhaled that morning told him so. Nasia came to sit next to him after a moment, asking him to show what he had written and poured out coffee for both. "Hey, it's your art fair today, when is it?" "Oh shit, yeah, art fair, it's around three in the afternoon, you want to go?"

It was 12 already, they looked at the wall-clock. "Then we don't have much time, let's get ready soon, after having breakfast of lunch, we'll be attending purity, with a pure soul like you." Earlier, she had been trying to convince herself that he was alright, but she could now hear it in his voice, the adrenaline rush in him, he had come back to his real life. "But you have not shown me that piece you are writing, and yeah, let me tell Samaira." She reached for her phone, informed her about the fair, and looked at him, telling her that he was back to being himself.

The fair was the most beautiful thing to be, between them especially, as it had been the starting of their story together, and he couldn't wait to create some destruction with his words. He got a notification from his publisher regarding his work they were about to publish. The level of ecstasy in Nasia was as high as the sight of an eagle, and she couldn't wait to get to the fair with him, with the Arav she had never seen, but was seeing now. Not thinking about anything else for a moment, she thought of calling Nash, but then she didn't. He decided to show her his written piece over their meal. At 2, they reach a cafe near the art fair, and had their food. He finally showed it to her and said, "Should I recite it, or let you both read it?" "Recite it, dear. It would sound far better than if we read it," said Samaira. He cleared his throat, sitting in-place and started:

Oh, how fool I see
in a mirror tarnished
for I write the birth of joy
for I smite the sorrow as destroy.
In the sheath of May
or the January holds
caught me to teach stay
and I unfold every folds.
Crawled since birth
walked since ever
every unsaid I heard
every step were clever.
Ask me to rejoin you in hell
heaven we create here
if lost I, play the warm bell
and you find me everywhere.

"I stopped there. When I looked at her this morning, I let every word evanesce in the air like the voices from last night." They were so into him, and realised that he had moved away from the voices and had dug a grave for them. Praising him for the words he had written and sharing joy together, they left for the fair.

It was so full of essence that morning, the morning that had brought them joy for the first time in so long, for the first time in all those years with his voice, he had not been with himself and was feeling the real presence of time with them, with the one he was in love with, the one who had brought him back to life, he was there wholly. Singing the songs of mirth and sharing their thoughts, he couldn't stop thanking Samaira for bring them in Paris, and now that he was living, really, and feeling his words too.

He thought of something that made him laugh real hard, and when asked why, he said, "Leave it, haha, it is just something shitty." But when they insisted, he said, "I was thinking, Nasia, why we never did it. Like, you create your art, and I write on your art, and then vice versa, what else could be the best weave? To create another world through your art and make meaning with my words?" he laughed again.

"Whoa, how did you even think about it and never told me anything like it before, why the hell did we never think about this earlier?" She felt so pulled, along with Samaira, by his idea, that yes, it was the alloy to be, so perfect, to create a new aura out of itself. In the fair and the exhibitions, where she would display her Art, his words could go along with it, describing it in more alive way. "Yeah, Arav, baby, it would be so perfect, living together and creating ruination together."

They reached the fair, it was set up at a huge scale. All the renowned collectors were there and she was one amongst them, a famous artist, who got approached by many when they recognised her face as they entered the fair, while Arav was back to his business, appreciating the beauty of each art, praising it, and Samaira, the one who had gifted art to her younger mirror, saw the collectors, met them and was on her way to meet her old friends there.

Nasia was being asked again and again about where she had been and why she took an off from her art. She had been asked so frequently to create something the art collectors could display, to create something for them, she took a break from all the hustle and went to Arav, they started interpreting pieces together, when a man named 'Paul Whites' came to them and confirmed if she was Nasia. When she said yes, he started, "Hey, I own galleries around the world, you must have heard my name in the sponsorship of so many events related to art. I want to offer you a chance to work for me on a project, you'll be paid well for it too, and it would be everywhere." He stopped to see her reaction, but she couldn't think of anything, as she had encountered the one who had once bought all the pieces worth millions of euros himself, on a project she had worked at, while Arav was looking at the personality of the gentleman.

"Oh, yeah, Paul, I have heard about you a lot, and if you want me to work for you, if you want unique results, then you'll have to give me time according to me, as art is not about given deadlines, but about emotions and everything. I will work on the project, but that's my thing, sir." Arav felt proud for her and the words she had said, whereas Paul got surprised and impressed to the level that he couldn't keep it to himself and said, "I am hearing this for the first time from someone who I have approached myself, and that's what I look for in everyone, unfortunately, there had been none, but now I think I have found the real holder of the project. You hold all the rights on this project from now on, I give you all the responsibility. There will be artists working under you now, the ones who have been working on it already. Congratulations, Nasia, my secretary will get in touch with you with all the details."

That morning was not only blissful for him, but for her too, as if the shower of spirituality was being sprinkled over her too. She accepted the offer, as to handle this project was the biggest thing she could ever have got. When Paul asked her about who she was with, she said, "a writer," as she knew that it was enough to describe him, "and my boyfriend."

He, Paul, got so confounded to come to know that. "Oh lord, what a pure texture you two made, to combine an artist and a writer, the most beautiful thing I have seen in a long time, bless you both. What if you work with he toor? Create an amazing world with your words? You must know how to play with them, it would be beneficial for me too, a description with beautiful words along with the art." Again, a blessing. "I would like to be called a poet first, then a writer, and yeah, I do just that, she creates a piece and I create words for her art."

"In that case, I need to double your profit. I guess, a poet, wow. I am not going to test you or see your work first as I believe her, so you should be together, there must be that colour of the untold in you. I can't wait to start with this new culture of art and poetry together, and you've got it, I offer you a place with her, Arav, congratulations." As if the mighty had come to the ground for them, they shared some more conversation, and after getting them both to sign the contract, he left.

After the fair, they celebrated their new beginnings over a small party and went to sleep a bit early, as they had their flight back to London the next day. It was as if the trip was planned by the almighty himself to give some lives a meaning. For Nasia, her opportunity to create and become the number one artist in the world, and for him, by creating something different and giving art another meaning, to change the stereotype. Paul's offer to him meant a change in the industry, which could lead to a whole new and wider beginning for them, whether it was for Paul, by taking the risk to change the industry, which could make him all the more famous and a great collector, or for Nasia, as she was a pure and gifted artist, her uniqueness was her weapon, and for Arav, the one who knew how to create another universe with his words, as the stars in the galaxy, and even for Samaira, who, after meeting her old friends, got to know her value in the industry, and was offered a place in event organisation as the head of the upcoming events in Netherlands.

They had embarked on a whole new journey, taking the old one along, a trip where a man learned to live again, learned of the reality by the power of love and care that he received, by both the sisters, and the new era, an old kind of new life, forgetting all the in-between years of his mental state, he had encountered himself, while Nasia got the offer to be the head of a project.

Some times, we don't know what is coming our way; being truthful to ourselves is the only way to live in this selfish human world. As for him, he never cursed anyone for his situation, but hung fire to be with reality, and she, who never cursed anyone for her life to be with someone like this, was now pure by having faith, and Samaira, who directed her younger image to be like her with ethics. This life-changing trip became everything between them, for them. What is gone, let it go, don't ever hold onto it again, for you still desire for it to happen again, but we must move on, we must not stop, for the sake of life, we must not feel despair, as the term itself wants you to be with it so that it can live through you. The right way is often right before us, all it needs is a sight of faith, pure belief, and most of all, truth and embracing. On their way back home, they were taking something robust away with them.

She couldn't wait to tell Aria about the big new offer, and how it could benefit their organisation, while Arav couldn't wait to meet his landlords, the old couple full of sheer love, and start with an old beginning he had left somewhere, because of his voices of destruction.

Chapter Nine

On the day of alluring breeze, he found himself in his zone, looking at his room, the sombre writings on his wall, nothing but shades of dark, he took some posters off and pasted new ones, full of bright words and having life in them. He soon got a call from the publisher again regarding his published work, maybe something to do with the review or feedback, he thought, and picked up the call with dirty hands, all messed up.

"Hey, Arav?" asked a familiar voice and so pulled up.

"Yeah, hi Sunny, how's it going?" He asked, curious about the work published by them, they had liked it, and Arav hoped that their readers would too. "I called you for this purpose only, the stats are booming with the new published words in our journal of 'Unpublished Voices' and I am sure you will be glad to find out that 'Voices Library' wants to hire you to work for us from now on." He heard it right, but he asked again, he heard the same, he couldn't contain the bliss he was feeling in him, what gave him more chills was not the news really, but that the people really liked his work. Taking the conversation further for a minute or two, he left everything and made a call to her.

Despite knowing that she might be asleep, he couldn't wait to talk to her. In fact, he was right, she was asleep, but not in her sleep, rather on her canvas, where she was creating something. She opened her eyes to his rings, thinking what it could be, she knew that he was alright but still couldn't let go of her concern for him so soon. "Hey, morning," she said. “I couldn’t wait to let you know about my publisher, they hired me and liked my work, and the thing that’s really dancing in me is that the readers liked it too.” Hearing his voice be so different than before, as well as the news, gave her the feeling of pure joy, she was really happy for him.

Waking up, she wiped her face and resumed her painting after the call, she had been so happy creating something, and when he told her that he was changing some of the posters in his room, it brought to her a breath of release as her efforts had not been wasted.

Samaira was to leave the next day for her work again, she felt her heart so heavy, but couldn’t do anything as it was her work. She had an early flight the next day, so they decided to meet in the evening that very day, where Aria was coming too, to meet and bid adieu for some weeks.

They meet at London bridge in the evening and went to have sushi, their favourite, after a long time, relating the stories from Paris to Aria. When she was told about Arav on the way, and was asked not to mention his transformation there even by mistake, she guessed that they had made love there, and Samaira, along with Aria, then started with their teasing game. Samaira remarked on the fading scar on Nasia’s neck, saying, “It’s faded now, but I saw it when it was as fresh as this coffee,” and made everyone burst out with laughter.

She hugged him before leaving and kissed him on the cheeks, telling him that she would be back soon, as she was only going to be away for some weeks, or hardly a month, and asked him to take care of himself till then, and her sister along with him, whose life had been given a whole new meaning. Arav wished her the same and said, “Miss me, but not much, I want to sleep too, haha.” While leaving, Nasia kissed him and Aria made a whispery hoot, waving him goodbye and goodnight.

It was all far too beautiful than before, he had left his dark past behind, the dark that had been smitten away by the brightness given by her, he continued his work of pasting new posters on the wall, and before going to bed, he left a love message to Nasia. He was off to sleep now in the night, that was really just a night now, unlike the dark of his life before.

Now that he had come back, he started going out more, meeting his landlords more often, when they asked the reason behind this positive change in him, and when he told them about her, they said, "Then we would like to meet that daughter who has changed my Arav to be so much more pure." "Oh surely, very soon, I'll tell her, haha." He also went back to sit in the park, writing and waiting to see the same old man and thank him. He was following his routine, until he got an event from Paul coming up, which got him busy writing on Nasia's pieces and making several revisions to serve the best. A day before the event, he went to the park again, to breathe some relaxation in as the last few weeks had been loaded for him. While sitting on the bench, Arav looked at the fountain and finally saw his old man in the evening, the man with his same old look, who stayed the same, not changing even with time. After days of spending his time visiting the park, in order to see him by chance, he finally did. Full of power inside, ignited to see him again, he stood up all of a sudden and walked towards him to talk to him again, to share his feelings and to tell him what an important role he had played in his life.

"Hey sir," he called out from behind, he looked rugged and in the same old jacket that had now got some patches on it, the hat was different today, he turned back to see who had called out, and took his hat off, trying to recongnise him. “Hey, the young man is here.” His unstable voice was even more off-track now, as if the blue of age had taken place, yet, he was still a vigorous old man, Arav noticed those wrinkles near his eyes and nose, thinking that he had aged so much so suddenly. “I am glad that you recognised me, sir,” he said stopping, while still noticing the changes he had made.

Making his steps towards Arav, still holding his hat tucked under his arm, he said, “Tell me, young man, how you have been lately?” while taking his seat on the bench facing the fountain. He took a deep breath, as if it had been a really long week for him as well. Arav told him about his life a bit, the trip to Paris and the changes that had come into his life due to Nasia. He did not mention his mental condition, but just the joys and memories. The old man heard it as if it was a story already written, and he was only hearing it again.

“Great, I am pleased to hear that from you,” he said and looked him straight in the eyes. Arav got a bit tensed when he said after a moment of silently smiling, “God bless you child,” as if relating to something hidden.

The old man looked quite changed to him today, more serious, but he gave himself hope that he might just have been helping others and someone like him came and interrupted him and made him furious, at the same time, he told himself to not think too much about it. When he asked the old man about it, he got up, placed his hat on the fence, and looked at the sky and then at the tree, as if he was trying to find something, someone. “What is it, sir?”

He tries to reach for the branch of a tree, but after two failed attempts, he stopped and looked at him, and said, “There was a bird I used to feed in the shade of the evening, when all the other birds got back to their shelters, that special one used to come here and sit on this branch and I fed her these biscuits." He took a packet out form his pocket, seeming oddly disturbed by something, something he was claiming.

"See there," he pointed to the visible roots of a tree, "There is one there, but she is not the one, she has a distinctive patch on her face, a patch of grey, not black, every other bird of her flock fears every one of us, they are so sensitive, but I somehow managed to gain this one's trust and we formed a magical bond, like the magical movement of our fingers," he stopped and moved his finger and asks him to do the same to feel the magic and beauty of it. Arav frowned at him and did what he had asked him to do. After a while, he interrupted him and said, "Sir, I might be wrong, but are you talking about squirrels? Cause the one you showed me was a squirrel." He laughed at him, as if he had just told him a really cool joke, he coughed and looked at him wordlessly smiling. A minute later he asked, "A squirrel? How will you make me believe that it's a squirrel and not a bird, and that they don't come out when it starts to get dark? For me, it is a bird and will stay a bird, for I have seen her like a bird and not a squirrel, that's my perception, right? It is my own and no one can ever take it from me, no one can take from anyone else their own insight towards everything. She will arrive for me, I know, she is just sad, I guess, for I didn't give her favourite food last time, walnuts." "Sir, I didn't get you. It's a squirrel, see, that one too, and there too, not a bird," Arav said, pointing around them. "And sir, why would you call them bird, when the species has been given the name of squirrel. They don't fly, birds do, they don't live in nests, birds do."

"That's what you think, just because they are called by some other name, doesn't mean that you can't name them something else. The bird that I am calling again and again, is a squirrel and not a bird, I know, but I call her bird, not by its species, but by the name that I have given her. Stop me as many times as you want, but for me it's a bird, because that's what I like to call them," he finally said, placing some biscuits for other squirrels before going back to sit at the bench.

"I am not getting a word you are saying. What is the reason behind it? What is it that you are trying to elucidate by this?" "To gain a squirrel's trust is so tough, you know? It only comes to those who gain it after a really hard struggle with their language of bond. As when I called her by the name of bird, you thought I am a fool to call a squirrel by something else."

He laughed again, "Young man," he whispered and said, "At times, what we see is not real, and for what we see real is not something that we don't want to see or cover in fiction. All I am saying is, what you think is real, is not always so, you need to change your perception for it to count." The old man got up, took his hat, and hailed at him as he left smiling and laughing. He was so confused, so benumbed to think, he looked at the tree again and then towards the old man, who had evanesced so suddenly, like the wind.

Arav, trying not to think about it too much for the sake of the event the next day, took the evening as a therapeutic walk and left a message to Nasia, before going to sleep, to wake him up the next day. In bed, he couldn't help but think about what had happened at the park, why did the old man say what he said and where had he vanished so suddenly, yet he tried to relax his nerves, and be prepared for the event the next day. He also decided to not tell Nasia about it. He took another deep breath and closed his eyes to fall asleep.

They decided to meet directly at the venue, as they would have gotten late, had they gone together. He had his coffee on the way, while she picked up something for him to eat, as she knew he wouldn't have had his breakfast, so she made him a sandwich, and left for the fair. All the thoughts from the previous day started occurring to him, he really believed in none of it, but this old man had said something that he didn't get, but swayed himself by believing that he had been touched by reality now and nothing must disturb his peace, that was given by her, he waited near the venue, waiting for her to arrive, he couldn't wait for a hug.

He saw her approaching, in a short black and blue jacket, with a basic white tee under, paired with washed denims and black boots. She had on that same beautiful smile with a natural untouched glow on her face. He opened his arms for her and she hugged him. He said, "Do I need to remark on your beauty today, cause I am falling short of words." "Haha, you don't need to, you already said it, baby. Did you have something to eat?"

"Oh no, I was getting late, I just had coffee, but it's okay, there must be something at the fair too." "No, I mean yeah, they might have something, but you would have to wait for too long for that. And I knew it," she said, taking out the sandwich she had made for him, "Here, this is for you, ass." He munched on it and then enquired where her art was. "Already in, Aria took it there last night." "Oh, Aria is in too, great." She asked him if he was prepared to speak on her piece, the words that he had written, as it would be the best time to impress Paul. "Yeah, I am." "I liked what you wrote."

Making their entry in, he saw a different fair today, more luxurious and fancy than any other that he had ever been to, but it was casual for an artist like her, as she got busy meeting her colleagues and introducing him to them as her boyfriend, which he really was. Then, Aria ran up to them, shared her love and told her that she had to be in the hall for a photo-op with her piece. They took Arav with them, but he said, "What will I do, dear, you should go, it's yours." "I don't care about that, we are here together and it will never be I alone, but we, with you, come with me, baby."

He was caught a bit off guard as he didn't know what to do with her there. He saw Paul standing there and smiling at him, gesturing a welcome. She held his hand for a photograph, as she had already mentioned as an intro on the wall of her art about him as the writer support. "When did you do that, that intro column?" "Aria did it, I told her to," she said, looking into his sparkling eyes.

It was so fancy, golden and white interiors and red carpets and more, he saw other art pieces by different artists when she told him to do so, as she had to go meet some of her art collectors and he insisted that he did not want to intrude. Words were running over his head to write and write, but he didn't, as he had already created a poem for the event. The time came for him to speak on her art, and they both were called on by the host, they looked at each other, she smiled and told him to say it as if he was only reciting it to her, for he was doing the same for her art. He spoke to the crowd and then looked at Paul, who was still smiling at him, longing to hear what he had written and for the reaction of other artists, as this was a new experimental practice. He took a step forward, closed his eyes, and pointed to her art, that was being displayed;

Lucidity -

Trembling with heavy thoughts,
Should I drawn or should I let go?
She fostered a defensive line, a line of hate;
So high to say a good-bye,
Dying to find herself on a bed, a bed of guilt, maybe.

She haunts me,
Screams: oh please, love me, love me, as she came.
Inaudible to everyone, but hidden under herself,
Cried to feel waking eyes.

Decided to left it unsaid,
If a mirror she read, to let it be unread,
She writes in her journals, I want to read the unwritten, can I?
Her eyes opening wider and wider, full off brims
and surprises as she came closer to
me, to my soul, to meet my inner and soon
I'll be gone.

I know, I know it's all messy,
But, she haunts me,
With her lust, lust to be loved.

He said it, feeling every word on his tongue like honey, in a way that sounded as the song of a Nightingale, everyone stood up and gave it a great applause, he looked at her, she came and hugged him, whispering, "You killed it, baby." They looked at Paul, he was so surprised to hear those words over that piece for the very first time in such a fair, which beautifully explained every inch of her piece. They got off stage, everyone praised her art and his words, when she got called by some of the collectors, she called him with her, but he said no again, for he wanted to see other art displays too.

Arav was looking at the piece named 'Aroma of my', and stopped to see the hidden in it, for the first time in all those years, he saw it without getting lost in himself, but in the piece, for he saw the reality of it, that showed the beauty of a murder within a murder of one, as the lad had portrayed on the canvas, bladed her throat and hung her pictures, while burning her room full of her blood. But when the ideology of reality hit him, the one by the old man that he hadn't told Nasia about, and didn't plan on telling her either, because he did not want to see her worry for nothing, he started tripping over his own words and brain, thinking whether the piece was the reality, or if it was the thing that was hidden in the fact of fibs. "Hey, Arav," called a voice he had never heard. He turned around to see an unfamiliar face, which he could partially remember from the crowd, from when he was reciting his piece. "Hi," he replied.

"I heard you recite your poetry, and it felt like the wind on the mountains and the shade of a tree, in the time of the heat of hate." He got zoned out to hear those words, and frowned, "That was so subtle, I didn't see that coming, haha, thank you for your graceful words, but who are you?"

"You're looking at my art, but did you not see the name?"

He looked at the name of the artist, and said, "Maya, Maya, is that you?" "Why would I ask you to read my name there otherwise?" "Haha, yes." "Whoa, it's really nice to meet you, Maya, and thanks for your words, the piece is so beautiful."

"What did you get?" "The reality, the fact that the lady there is being murdered by the murder of her own, the contrast and the picture is so dark, yet soothing."

"It's not always what you see, dear, you got it right that it is a murder into a murder, but did you see that later murder of that burning room into a new life on the floor?" He saw the piece again and spotted what she had said.He had taken it to be a chair, but it was actually a lady, getting bigger and bigger. "Yeah, I just saw it; I thought it to be a chair." He was stunned.

"Never trust your eyes and let your inner self decide your sight, keep it in your mind to live the un-lived." He didn't know what to say any further, as she had caught him by her untouched beauty. His heart told him not to indulge with her anymore for it could end in something else, when she flicked her hair back and looked into his eyes, smiling with that perfect shade of black lipstick. "I would like you to meet my girlfriend. Could you wait here for a minute, please? She is right there," he said, pointing at Nasia, where she was talking to Paul. "Oh, is she your girlfriend? Another artist herself, yeah sure." He smiled and left to summon her to meet this lady, who had caught his thoughts with her reticent words.

When he went to call her, Paul gestured at him to not speak a word. Nasia and Arav kept standing there quietly, while he looked through some papers, he was not looking too happy at that moment, but was frowning and serious. He gave them a paper and when they read it, Nasia almost shed a tear to see what a great big deal the organisation had offered both of them, Arav and herself. "Sorry to scare you both, haha, oh my lord, it's a contract for a new project, for you both are now my new permanent senior members of the team. You did so great that I can't even describe it by my own, I am so stunned and it shook me to see the love and understanding between you too." They talked for a while before Paul left, saying, "I'll meet you both very soon with another event to kill, haha, I need to leave for some meeting now."

Nasia was so happy to see that she had done something really big for her organisation and for them, and they shared the pure joy of it. Just then, he looked back and saw Maya looking at him with the same look, a smile as enchanting as an illusion of a foregone path, her eyes were the shade of the sky in black. "Oh Nasia, I wanted you to meet someone I just saw, what a piece she has done, and she really wants to meet you too." "Oh me? Haha, who is she? where?" He pointed at Maya, but she had left, he saw her leaving urgently. "Where, baby?" "Oh, I think she is gone, someone must have called her, I just saw her leaving." "Oh, haha, its okay, tell me when you see her again."

He felt a little nervous and shamed of himself as he had made her wait and so she had left saying nothing, a guilt grew in him, as he really wanted them to meet. He also couldn't really get over her words on reality, and started contrasting her theory with the old man's theory on it, he had started to feel so trapped in himself, when Nasia came to him and asked, "What did you guys even talk about?" "Oh nothing, just about her piece that I tried to understand, but failed by one thing only, haha." "Haha, you fail too? I never knew, it's okay, you never failed to understand me, haha."

Meeting with some new faces at the fair through Nasia, who claimed everywhere that he was the one she was in love with and added the tag of a 'writer' to his name whenever someone asked what he did. The fair was about to end and he was craving for a coffee to calm his nerves and stop the thunders that were going through him. "Do we need to stay here?" "Oh no, we are already done. Let's get something, yeah? You must be hungry, love, and I think it's coffee that you are craving for, haha." They waved a final good-bye to the people there, and on their way to a nearby restaurant, she told him about her art, how a collector wanted to purchase a previous piece and how he had really been trying to get in contact with her. He tried his best to respond to whatever she was saying, but something caught his attention, it was not the lady, but the old man's words about everything he had said the previous evening.

In a restaurant with Sufi music playing, they talked and talked about the event, and Paul, and their future of how they could get a lot through this, to start a life of luxury, better than they had been living, and then the publisher who had hired him for real. "What you going to write, have you got anything?" "Not really, but yeah, I think it would be something about unrequited love maybe, let's see." After an hour, they left. She wanted him to stay with her that day, or to go to his place to stay with him, but there was something worrying him. He said, "Yeah sure, if you want to," and smiled at her. "Let's go to my place? For my landlords have been wanting to meet you too, ever since I told them about you, so we can go there in the morning." "Yeah sure, that would be so beautiful, gee, I am excited, haha," she said, jumping like a child. They make their way towards his home to spend the night together.

It felt so pure in his room when she entered it, she felt a whole new kind of aura, an aura of something more positive and more alive, with the new posters on the wall and how everything was exactly at its place. She whispered within that she has done it, she knew it, but it gave her a real breeze of ease to see that he was finally being himself. He forgot everything when she held his hand and showed him how much she loved him; he said the same too, being there with her, only her.

A night full of fireflies, under the sky with naked stars, on top of the mountain with each other perfectly as soft as grass in the fields, the same wind that came touching the trees and the garden of hills to their faces. Her head rested on his chest and he tried to figure out how many hair she even had on her head, but lost count again and again, while she was busy listening to his heartbeat rushing inside him. It was the night of love, a night of sheer love under one roof, where it felt like the same.

Waking up early, she left his home to get ready and come back to meet his landlords. While leaving, she said, “Oh, you once told me something about an old man too, will we meet him as well?” “No,” he almost screamed, “No, I haven’t been able to spot him in the last few days, he might be too busy helping others as he did for me by revealing his fake theory of reality.” “What do you mean by a fake theory?” “Oh, I mean, he is unique, haha.” “Okay, I’ll be back soon, be ready on time. Sometimes it feels like I am the man and you, the lady in our relationship, haha.”

In the bliss of the morning, he looked out the window after she left, and saw the old man standing near a tree, trying to figure out something by touching and looking at it as if he was about to climb it and then jump from the very top. He didn't think even once this time to run and talk to him, as he used to do earlier, cause of that evening, the very ideology of the facts and reality he believed in, got duped by the same old man who had saved him several times. He didn't know whether he should really tell Nasia about it, but his other brain said no, as it was not something unreal and he was committed to live in the reality and out of his imagination now. He walked away from the window and went to take a shower, where he laid his sight on the mirror at his own image, and out of the blue, Maya's words on the same thing came to him mind all of a sudden, all the while he took showering, he was not with himself but with the thoughts of Maya, and her beauty that had captured him, but he let it go by telling himself that she and her thoughts were to him, as Nasia had said, "Believe it, if you want to, let it go, if you find it shit, I'll believe in you every second." He recalled her words to let himself not get distracted by any others, such as Maya. She was a good artist and he would surely stop to meet her if he saw her in any other art fair.

While he was putting on his clothes, the bell rang. He went to take the door, while still wrapped in a towel. "Look at you, haha, what the hell were you doing? Your hair is all dried now, how long have you been sitting there with no clothes on? Haha." "Haha, baby, haha, it is just that I found a book and wanted to see what's in there, as I've never read it before and it distracted me and I got so involved in it that I forgot I had picked it up just to see and not to read, haha." He put on his clothes and after giving her the kiss she had been waiting for, they leave off to meet his landlords as a surprise visit on a Friday. She asked what all he had told them about her. He replied, "Really not much, it was them, in fact, who noticed a different charm of calm in me and guessed there there was someone new in my life, and it's you dear."

She hid behind him when they reached their door, with a big beautiful mixed bouquet of roses, lilies and daffodils, along with a box of chocolates. he rang the bell and Mr. James came to take the door this time. The glow on his face doubled with joy, he hugged him and remarked how happy he always got every time he saw him, even if it was as frequently as some days apart. Arav moved aside to reveal Nasia standing behind with the huge bouquet, which she offered to Mr. James. He looked at her frowning, but before he could even ask anything, she spoke, "I am Nasia, sir, and I've heard about you and your wife a lot." "Oh, whoa, you are the one who have created a saga out of him, a short story, come in, welcome dear." He took the bouquet and kissed her hand, welcoming her in. Mrs. Walsh was watching the TV. "Love my love, your charm has arrived to meet you with someone really beautiful." She turned around and was spellbound for a moment to see the bouquet, and her glow and his smile. She stood up and said, "Arav, my love, come, wow, is she the one you were talking about?" Nasia blushed red and offered the box of chocolates to her. She frowned a bit at all of them and then said, "Oh, my innocent child, I think he didn't tell you whom to give what, haha." Nasia couldn't understand her and they all burst into laughter, "Baby, those flowers were meant for Mrs. Walsh and the box of chocolates for Mr. James, haha." "Why didn't you tell me this before, Arav, oh I feel so embarrassed now, haha." "Because I wanted to enjoy this very moment."

"Sorry, I was just so nervous, haha." "Oh my child, it's okay, men play this way with us." Over a cup of coffee and some snacks, they chatted as a family, sharing love, while she appreciated the beauty of the old couple, feeling that what Arav had told her about them was indeed true. Mr. James talked about his stories, how he used to be before her and the charm she had, while Mrs. Walsh claimed that he was flattered by her, and they talked endlessly with joy. Almost three hours passed away while they talked and played games like chess, jenga and dumb-charades, a day which gave them hope of more beautiful days ahead. When they were about to leave, Mrs. Walsh said, "You both now have to come here more often together, and thank you for the gifts, dear, this young man is good for only coffee, haha." "Haha, yes Ma'am, I surely will, and it felt so good to have spent this time with you, I can't even describe it now.

The old couple was so happy to have met the lady of Arav's life. They had already had a lot of food there and when she asked him to meet the old man again, he said, "He won't be there, baby, I know, it's as if he is bound by days there, a day he is there, then the next, at a different place." Clearly, he didn't want her to meet him at that point, as he wanted to figure the complexity of it out first. She didn't guess that he was hiding something at all. "Oh, okay, I got you, haha. Thank you, Arav, it feels like I have met someone of my own after meeting them, they are so pure."

Dropping him outside his home and giving him a kiss for goodnight, she left. Everything was so perfect, but again, when the term arrived to him, it took something very odd with it. He remembered her charm and the days spent with her and other people too, in order to not think about anything else that was worrying him, as it was shifting so frequently form the old man to Maya, and then the charm and essence of her.

Days passed by, weeks after weeks, they started working together on the new project and started spending more days together too, sometimes at his place, and at times at hers, while he also started to write to his publisher on unrequited love, which was all getting published the same time as he was sending it to him. Nasia's art was reaching different heights too, getting sold at very high prices and creating a disaster at every new piece that it went to, she has earned a name for herself at a very high level in her industry.

Finally, after more than a month, Paul organised another art fair, they had attended many until then, but none by him. Arav had something to recite on stage, not the second time, but perhaps more than the tenth. But the piece he has written for this event was more of him, where she had created something like a fantasy or fiction of the illusion of life, he had written about life as an illusion, it was relevant enough, but she didn't know if it was reflecting of a personal level of his.

On Sunday, May 7, 2017, it was a new day for them, as he had written something very different this time to recite on stage, separate from her art, and was also hoping to see Maya again, so that he could tell her that she was wrong somewhere in her theory of reality. The event was two days later, yet they were all prepared, the art had been sent to the venue, and he was prepared to recite a poetry on illusion for the first time. He did not spend the night before the event with her, as he wanted some space for his mind to be calm and perform as best as possible and make it sound as beautiful as Nasia, and her art.

The night sky was full of starless clouds that night, he was there again, under his roof, but the wind was not blowing like it really should have been, it was not because she was not with him tonight, but he could write the saddest lines tonight, not for his beloved, but for the reality he was living, a corrupted race of facts. Tripping down his memory lane again, the old man and Maya appear, he should have been happy with this new venture, but he was not, he was even more sad about the next day, drowning in his own melancholy to even recite the piece. Why was he going to recite it at the fair, if it was not going to giving him any joy anymore? All he knew was that he loved Nasia a lot, and he couldn't let her go, but why were all such thoughts coming to him?

Not thinking about it anymore, he went to sleep with a heavy head. Craving for Nasia's touch, he went off to sleep, while writing over his tongue the saddest lines of that night, that he was not living in her joy, but in the pain of his own self, why?

Chapter Ten

Arav spent a whole day with him, talking to her at times for some hours and writing for his publishers, and consuming the rest of the time thinking about the next day, there was an aura of intrusion surrounding him, then lines on his forehead barely disappeared for more than a few minutes. Before going to bed that night, before waving a goodnight kiss to her over the video call, he lay his hand over the diary, the old diary of truth, to set it in its place on the shelves, and covered himself with a blanket, like a child waiting for morning to arrive.

The special day finally arrived, the new day when she had to showcase her dry-point abstracted art, along with his poetry on illusion, for the very first time. They walked in together on the red carpet that was chiefly matted for guests and artists like themselves, met with Paul, who was really excited to see a new era of her side and was excited about the words he had never heard. "Are you alright, babe? You seem a bit changed since the last time I saw you." "Oh, it's nothing, I am just a little nervous maybe, for it's the piece of reality that I am going to recite over your beautiful destruction through the very idea of illusion."

All the time, he felt lost somewhere, despite being with her, and looked around to catch a sight of the lady of enchantment by chance, but he didn't. The sense he had at that moment, being there with so many voices, yet he could hear none, just his own breaths and the colourless rainbow colours. Making their presence in the hall of display and exhibition, to see others' art too, they did not see any comparative to hers, mainly because it was along with the words of a poet. Holding his hand, she tryied to get into him, but couldn't, as he had fostered that line of defense so as not to let her cross over into his inner, while she let it be, thinking that he was only getting anxious, waiting to recite and would be okay as soon as this got over.

Aria got on stage and called them over to talk and reveal the words of his inner self. They walked over to her hand in hand, she said some words on her art, while he just appreciated her sheer beauty, her words, her perfect lips letting the words out of her throat, and her hair flowing down in the curls of prose that she was wearing, Nasia had noticed, however, that he was not completely alright, he was not himself, but she couldn't understand what it was and decided to talk to him after he recited his words. He stepped further and took the mic after she had showed them her piece and told them half of what it meant, the rest being left to him to describe in his words.

He looked at the crowd, as if he was looking at them for the last time, holding tears in his eyes, he looked for Maya but failed again. "Murder, murder," he said and started:

As I see, I sight the frightening frown,

In the lust of lust being here,

Death a mortality, may you immortal,

For death is alive and alive is dead.

And the sour oh sour taste of sweet,

Crave I thee,

Rarely do I breathed of self,

May thou been, June I be.

The rasps within, alas!

How I did not betoken April of trust?

Rover of pain we are,

End of sundry ends; life renders.

Ashes of cosmic blues,

Dramatic rose to sully a piece of my,

Oh the life of good-bye I live,

In void of hopeless prays, let I die.

His voice started breaking and the stammers became clear as he stopped the second he saw her in the middle of the crowd, her eyes crying black kohl, being red, where the lipstick of blue seemed shattering like the pieces of a mirror, naked, laughing at him, so hard that only he could hear her voice and none other, in the middle it was so loud, he looked at her closely and then at others, thinking why they couldn't feel her presence. 'Maya,' he screamed within, while everyone stared at him, waiting for him to say further, while he was lost in her smile and let his tear fall freely, who was marring her beauty being still, naked in the nudity of death. "Maya," he said on the mic. Nasia was dismayed to see him like that, when she followed his gaze, she found that there was nothing there. After a second, he continued, with red eyes and a drop of pain:

Again, vow me no promises,

What a language of November thou speak?

Summer, spring, fall of winter days?

Long me no longing of body of adultery,

Naked it stands in the middle,

Black tears and red throat,
Murderer, murderer the body screams,
With blood oh blood, a story she wrote.

Death fear me, life not,
As dark as humans I stay,
Truth, their screech in calls,
Facts no fetched, and in hate of curse I lay;
Corrupt the race of humans,
For innocence of a lamb they killed,
Grave; in grave murdered truth is,
Poesy of dark may the old rebuild.

He had kept his eye on her, who kept laughing and laughing with tears of black and blood, he took the mic down and smiled at her.

As soon as he finished it, he looked at Paul, who really had no idea about what he had just said, but knew that it was a complete success anyway. He walked towards Nasia and kissed her to taste the soul and to remember. Hearing a loud applause from the public, he thanked them with a gesture and left the hall without waiting for Nasia. She didn't know how to react or what had even happened to him all of a sudden, but when he left, she nearly ran after him to catch him, but got caught by another artist herself. "I'll be back in a while, please excuse me, I need to do something important, if you will please allow me..." "Yeah, sorry, and sure, we are here."

Arav has gone off the grid, while she was going crazy looking for him in everyone, losing her mind and sanity. When Aria saw her in this condition, she got real worried for both of them and started looking for Arav with her. She felt all the more messed up, her eyes grew more and more red and her pale, as she realised that they were getting nowhere, she didn't think of anything but only his love, who was in a big problem and she couldn't let it happen. She lost it totally when she finally screamed in the aura of silence and the fancy of art, "ARAV!" Everyone stopped to look at her blankly running and searching for him in the corners of the venue. "ARAV, PLEASE ANSWER!" They got to know then, that something was not right. She cried again and Aria tried her best to control her at that moment of sole consciousness to find him.

She was taking it on herself, only herself, blaming herself for nothing really, but to find him and talk to him right away was all that mattered to her, even if it took her breath away. "ARAV, I AM GETTING OUT OF BREATH NOW." Thinking that he would definitely reply now, for he couldn't take her to be so, she didn't realize in her innocence that someone else's breath had already come down to five percent. She had known from the very moment that she met him that day, that something was not good with him, but he had created a line of his smile which prevented her from coming to know of anything.

"What the fuck was I thinking, Aria? Tell me, I should have stopped him right when he got off the stage, it's all my vice, how foolish could I be, to not read behind his words and think that he was out of everything and had embraced the factuality of subconscious." Nasia hugged Aria with refreshed tears which grew all the more frequent. "Nothing will happen, dear Nasia, believe me, its okay, baby, I am here with you, he is fine."

When the crowd started chattering about her condition, unaware of the thing that was going on with them, Paul ran to her and held her from her shoulder, trying to make her believe that he would be fine and that he must be somewhere. He might not have known anything, but he knew not to ask any stupid questions. Instead, he asked, "Have you checked the rooms?" "Paul, I have checked nearly everywhere, help me, please," she said, collapsing within, but maintained her sanity for the need of the hour. Just then, two guards came running to them and said that they had found someone upstairs in the hall, lying on the ground and foam coming out of his mouth. They rushed upstairs, all out of their breaths. When they reached the hall and saw him on the ground, the foam of poison coming out of his mouth, Nasia rushed to him screaming his name and crying out loud.

On her knees, she took his head on her lap, screamed to call for an ambulance, wiped out the white foam from his mouth, he was nearly smiling to see her, she again shouted to pick him up for the hospital, but he somehow managed to move his lifeless hand to her mouth and said, "I am done, nothing can save now, let it be, I don't have much time, Nasia, talk to me." "Shut the fuck up," she screamed at him, "Shut up, you have a life now, you are not going anywhere." He struggled to say, "Don't be a kid, talk to me. Move away, move away from us a screech of shipwreck."

With a strangulated voice, he said, "I loved you so much and it will only grow stronger and stronger eternally, till I meet you there again," and asked her to take a paper out of his pocket. He smiled and said to her, "Now that you have touched me, I am leaving, to meet you again," with his eyes red, and tears all over his face.

Looking into her eyes, laying in her lap and keeping the last eye contact, his breathed, as if looking for the key she held in her eyes to unlatch the door and leave. He was cold earlier, but now grew colder, she felt his breath on her face, the exhale of sheer cold, as if he was touching her for the last time with his soul, and had now turned into just a meaningless body, laid in the questioning milieu. For a moment she thought that he was there with her, holding onto her hand tightly still, but when she saw no further response, she crumbled and fell apart in pieces. "You can't do this, Arav, listen!" Her voice grew more and more bleak, calling out to the lifeless body of Arav, but can you call out to a body having no soul in it?

She did not let anyone touch either of them, while screaming her throat out, "Move away, move, don't dare to come near." She then looked at the paper she had received as a last token by him. She opened it to reveal two sheets; one seemed like a letter, while the other just had some lines. She took the letter down and read the second one, on which it was written:

"Every time, before the dawn and after the skyline, I thought it's easy that way, the way I was living, hiding myself to myself, for the good of my own. When you asked me about the old man, I had got to know just a day before that the man who had saved my life several times with his theories, never really existed, and the lady I asked you to meet at the fair, Maya, just as her name suggests, was just another illusion of my attempt to get a hold on life like yours. How could I ruin the beauty of an angel?

The old man and Maya never existed, just like Anvisha and Manik, but Grace was there, alive, the one I had thought to be as dead as me.

Accept, I do, all your sins, but to live the sin by living only for myself is no greater than breaking a heart of my whole, Nasia. Forgive me, if you can, in the land of ours, I will stay, to guide the life of my whole."

She gasped. All that time, she thought that he had been embraced by reality and he did too, but that his own brain would play tricks and illusions to bring him this way, she had never thought. She looked at Aria, crying, lost with her and gave that paper to her to read, while Nasia opened the other. Spots of dried tears of Arav were everywhere, this was a letter, a letter for his beloved, her, her and only her, Nasia.

"The bright, I still remember the bright that made a dawn sigh. I remember everything, and each of your words I am taking with me for I can't take anything with me, but only the essence of your touch and your words, like magic, I heard all the time from those lips of yours that I have tasted, that relish I am taking with me today. All these years, life lived me cleverly, now in my time, it's only my stamp, for the first time, let me be clever to take everything of yours, that ignited a scintilla in my eyes, with me.

Oh, how am I going to make my life up there without you?

I am going to close my eyes and pretend to be dead as being alive, to live in your eyes in the night time when you look at the stars, searching for me, you don't need to, just close them and feel me within when a wind touches you, that would be me, and if in daylight you want to see me, look out the window, for in every bird, I'll live for you, if you ever want to smell me, crave me, smell the coffee.

I know, I did no good, that you holding this last piece of paper of my words in your hand, is like you holding my breaths with it. Every night, I'll be visiting you, every time, I'll be watching you, because to be on the ground there, with life, I was not living, but just being used by these illusions, for them to thrive.

Now that I am as cold as stone, I'll be waiting, waiting for you every single second, and there would be only one name in each of my breath, Nasia, and I'll breathe it to wait for you. Even if have to fight with the almighty for you, I will kill myself again and again, till I find my way to you, up here, to make him realise that he has to listen my voice, my words, to send my beloved to me, or see me dying again and again forever. He will have to bring you to me, for he would know that you want the same too.

Don't cry for me, it's not worth it, for we'll be together up here, feel your breath, I am there.

Waiting for you, waiting to be touched by an angel; My Nasia."

Having read the last words, she looked at him and kiss his forehead and then his lips. She collapsed, her eyes getting blurry and more so by seeing his eyes, which were still looking at her, but dark now.

She opened her eyes on the hospital bed, and saw Samaira and Aria standing at her side, holding her hand. She had been unconscious for a day, and they had started to get really worried about her. When she opened her eyes, they heaved a sigh of relief. Nasia looked at her sister, trying to speak, to vent her words out, but she couldn't, overwhelmed by a feeling of weakness and incapability to talk. Instead, she let her tears fall free. "Shh, shh, no baby no, you don't need to say anything, you are not bound to, not now, after a while you can, I am here with you now."

The next day, she was discharged to go home. All that she had spoken during this whole time was, "Arav, I want him. It's all my fault." Samaira and Aria stayed together to take care of her during that critical state of her break down. She refused to speak to anyone after that incident, she wanted to cry, but it was all kept inside, and even when she wanted it to, it didn't come out. They were told to not force her for anything, and that she would start talking by herself, but they did all they could to make her laugh, everything, every moment they tried to make her laugh by talking to her, but she didn't speak a word, didn't even look at them, and when she did, it was just a sight of a colourless rainbow. They were worried about her, but all they could do was wait, wait for her to come back from this reserved Nasia.

Ten days passed without her having spoken a word, she did not even go out of her room much, and when she did, it seemed as if they had an alive corpse in the house, insane, she didn't know anything, but when she finally went near the window on the tenth day and saw the birds outside, she smiled and said, "You were right, you are here, haha." They were standing in the lobby observing her and worrying about her, but when they heard her cheerful words upon seeing the birds fly, they were surprised. She turned around to look at them and said, "See? He is here. He told me that he would live for me in the birds, look there." Samaira ran up to her and hugged her, while she continued to smile, seeing Arav in those birds. "Don't worry, haha, I am alright," she said. She then took a jar of coffee in her hands and smelled it as if she would fill her lungs up with it. Aria, after a while, took the jar from her hand. She protested, "What? Let me smell him, he is in there, you can smell him too!" She then ran back to her room and slept, covering herself under a blanket. They could not leave her alone, as every day since she had come back, they were sleeping with her, cuddling her death like person.

In her room of despair, melancholy and dejection, she slept every night to wait for that one moment, she prayed and chattered in her mind, breathing Arav's name the whole time. Like every night, Nasia woke up that night out of her blues again to see her sister and Aria sleeping with her, but it was not what it seemed, for she saw herself asleep there too.

Moving out of her body, which was on the bed with them, she saw Arav's hand calling her to go to him with no delay.